Run Throug

By

William Clark

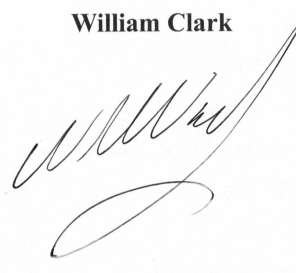

"Watching someone dance looks insane, only if the witness does not hear the music." Von Richt, 1756....

Table of Contents

Chapter One - Flashes

Staff Sergeant Bruce Lattimer went through the pre-shot sequence just as he had a thousand times before. This time, however, the weapon before him was as far from the Barrett 82A he used as an over-watch hitter in Iraq as Texas is to the moon. The new weapon had passed several years of extensive lab and field trials at the DARPA facility in Northern Virginia, and this would be its first real-world mission. He trained his eye down the sight-line. The wind would not be a factor for the shot, nor would the air temperature or the risk of collateral damage. Now, all he had to do was ignore the onion breath of the young DARPA tech watching the target through a pair of binoculars lying on the ground next to him.

Lattimer didn't know anything about the chosen target, had never met the man before. That choice had been made light years above his position. The guy making his way around a pickup three-hundred-twenty meters south by southeast was it.

Lattimer checked the optics, still amazed that he wouldn't have to adjust for bullet drop or windage. He could make a dead-on shot to a point on Mars if he aimed the laser at it. Settling into a comfortable prone position behind the gun, he whispered into the bone mic. "Ready in two mics." He began to slow his breathing, willing himself into relaxation. The world outside the illuminated sight slowly fell away as he watched the man downrange through the ten-fixed veritable scope.

He was in his familiar pre-shot routine. The distractions were gone. The only thing he heard now was his breathing. Gone was the onion breath and the small rock under the shooting mat that was digging into his elbow. The mental and physical aspects of high-level shooting were all now in focus. This needed to be a frontal headshot with the target looking directly at him - laser tag with a million dollar price. He took the weapon off "safe" with a slight movement of his thumb and whispered the word "*ready.*"

Hearing the command, the spotter, another sniper Lattimer had never met before, turned on the L-RAD sound emitter ten meters off to his right. The small dish-like device, about the size of a large dinner plate, could send three one-second chirps in the 30 kHz decibel range a distance of fifteen hundred meters. The chirps, also directed by laser, would be loud enough to make the target turn to the noise, setting up the frontal shot.

"*You have the control,*" whispered the spotter over the radio. "*Whenever you're ready.*"

Lattimer slowly put the tip of his index finger on the weapon's wide trigger and took up a slight bit of trigger-creep. A heartbeat later, the 30 kHz sound cannon fired three loud chirps and the man downrange suddenly turned towards the noise. Lattimer fired.

At the speed of light, the green 7mw military-grade laser shot across the desert hitting the target in the face with pinpoint accuracy. Within a nanosecond, a 1.5 GB blast of implanted memory information instantly imprinted in the neural network of the brain, deep in the cerebral cortex. As if frozen, the target stood in stunned silence, watching the incredible implanted hallucination appearing before him. He would never be the same.

Lattimer kept his scope on his target for a moment longer, suddenly feeling a pang of guilt for having made the shot. The man who stood two hundred meters away in a trance was not an enemy combatant, not some radical jihadist bent on the country's destruction, not even an enemy of the State.

This was not the mission he had signed up for. He was now part of a machine that took things away from people - freedom, possessions, the right to choose, and now, the ability to distinguish reality from mind-blowing illusions.

This human lab rat, picked out of the general American population just because the shot callers could do it, was just a regular guy out for a ride in the desert on his dirt bike. With nothing more than a shaft of light, his life had changed course for good. Talk about being in the wrong place at the wrong time. Killing him outright would have been far more merciful.

For the first time, the unfairness of it all hit Lattimer just above the heart making him feel like he was leaving the scene of a crime as he turned to leave. He hopped into the waiting helicopter and made a vow to himself. "There will be no more domestic black ops. The Army and the Agency will just have to deal with it. I'm done. If leadership doesn't like it, they can go fuck themselves. Twenty years is enough." This one had left a bad taste, one that would be there for a long time - maybe forever.

***

Clay Carson had no idea what he had seen. Hell, he didn't even know how to process the images that had been repeating in his head since yesterday.

The trip that he had taken to the desert, a planned mental reboot from the crazy last three months of work, had turned into something he couldn't have expected in his wildest dreams. He sat in his truck motionless, the sun just starting to rise in the east, casting a deep purple-orange glow across the open horizon.

He hadn't slept all night, hadn't even opened the door to the new tent he bought last week at Wal-Mart. He looked to his left at the bright yellow and blue two-man structure rippling gently in the early morning breeze. *"W/speed>8 k"* The equation flashed across his mind's eye, jolting him from his trance. He adjusted himself in the seat, suddenly realizing that he was still wearing his dusty motocross pants, boots, even his riding gloves. Trying to clear his head, he pushed open the truck door and stiffly, for the first time in almost fifteen hours, stepped out.

He had lost track of the number of times he had come to the Mojave to ride motorcycles with his father. It had been a series of shared adventures that began when he was only a kid. The desert was their refuge, a place for emotional healing for them both. When the old man died three years ago, he kept making the trips. It was still their time, a way he could maintain the connection.

This was familiar ground - this campsite, or at least it had been yesterday. Now, there was a palpable difference hanging in the breeze, like the lingering tone when loud music is suddenly turned off. The air was electrified with that last lingering note. Things were different. He was different.

As he slowly worked to process things, he suddenly felt an incredible surge of energy and a growing sense that he should be moving. The overpowering need to get to somewhere, somewhere important, was so intense that, for a moment, he considered just leaving his bike, the tent, and the rest of his camp gear where they sat.

As he quickly pushed the motorcycle up the loading ramp into the back of his pickup, his mind raced with the weight-to-mass ratio of the motorcycle, the angle of the ramp, the pounds-per-square-inch of force it took to move it, and the weight he and the bike exerted on the truck's suspension. The flood of information presented as a visual torrent of numbers and equations in his mind's eye, a stream of consciousness unlike anything he had ever experienced before.

He stared at the bike, realizing that for every motion, every body movement, related equations, and statistical facts flooded his mind. He felt like a machine, an advanced computer, becoming conscious of its environment.

He took a moment and watched the sunrise as if for the first time, taking in the first shafts of golden rays of light cresting the horizon. *How will I explain this,* he thought, hopping over the side of the truck, landing *4 feet 5 inches from the ground, mass on impact - 200-foot pounds per square inch, greater than .1 g-forces on legs. Ecto compression greater than 000.2.* The data flashed across his mind in a nano second.

He knew there would be questions, anger, and confusion from family and friends who would not understand who he was now. "Not important," he said aloud, sliding in behind the steering wheel. Judgment and opinions on what he now had to do would mean nothing.

The overwhelming need to be in motion pushed him as he dropped the truck in gear, spun out of the campsite and onto the highway's access road in a dusty slide, his mind a blur of equations and conversions - distance in miles, kilometers and yards to his destination, truck acceleration, speed, and RPMs. It was all so clear, so stunningly clear that he laughed out loud at its thoroughness. "My God!" he shouted through the tears as he held the wheel in a grip of *9.2 pounds.* "My God!"

***

A hundred and seventy miles northeast of Boston on Penobscot Bay is the small New England fishing town of Stonington, Maine, formerly a wind-lashed settlement known as Green's Landing. The town was named for the granite quarries that once provided steady work for the populace, quarries long since closed, leaving the need to supplement the moderate fishing business with growing tourism.

Most of the hard-edged locals grudgingly accept the migration of sight-seekers who arrived every summer to enjoy the quaint town. As far as Bing Duchene, a fourth generation Lobsterman was concerned, he would gladly take every dollar the well-heeled Bostonian tourists wanted to spend on New England charter-fishing and charm, but to him, there was nothing charming about the bare-knuckle living he made from the sea. The ocean wasn't a romantic but a wicked bitch that would drown you - wreck your boat and break your back on the rocks if given half the chance. It was the cold-hearted killer he faced every day, an adversary that had taken his father, two brothers, and a cousin back in ninety-eight.

His father's boat the *Anna Durbin,* a fifty-five foot Provincial twin-engine, had gone down in rough seas somewhere near *Isle au Haut,* one of the small rocky islands off the coast. He hadn't been on the boat when they left harbor that day because he had severed his little finger in a rolling hoist block two days before. The last transmission he received from his father was that they could see the Lighthouse on Robinson point and were making a turn for the lea side, trying to outrun some heavy weather that was starting to hammer in. There had been no distress call after that, no witnesses as to what happened - nothing. The Anna Durbin, the gear, and the four-man crew simply vanished as if they had never existed. The injury to his little finger had saved his life.

He looked down at the little finger where he gripped the ship's wheel. This was the last day of his three-day run along the south bank. He had pulled all of his traps, filled both tanks, and would be back at Stonington Harbor just after dark, a return trip that could not come soon enough. Fishing the waters where his father and brothers were lost always gave him the yips.

He knew the currents, the water temperature, and the bottom features of the area, but for the last two days, an unexplained and building anxiety about being out there had taken hold. Jack Tatum and Billy Haas, the other two members of his crew, had picked up the Captain's vibe and were doing everything they could do to stay quiet and out of his way.

A thick rain-wind combination from the east had picked up right at sunset, darkening the mood on the boat even more. Billy rolled up the last of the Spinner leads and trap weights in the barrel and then flicked his cigarette over the side.

"Jesus Christ, it's getting cold!" he shouted over the wind at Jack on the other side of the rain-soaked deck. The older man was securing the boom lines on the trap hoist with quickness and strength that belied his mid-sixty age.

Like Billy, Jack was a generational Lobsterman, having spent most of his life on the cold-water deck of a fishing boat. That's all he knew. That's all he wanted to know.
To him, life on shore was just a whole lot of bad noise, crazy ex-wives wanting money, bill collectors wanting even more money, and shit-for-brain tourists who clogged the bars and restaurants, ran the few stop signs, and generally screwed up life for those who lived in Stonington year-round. On the water, life made sense - do your job, stay off the downline, don't foul the prop, and don't fall overboard – all easy rules to live by.

As he tied down the final trap and pulled his hood tight against the rain, he thought of how you could do all those things on nights like this and still not make it home. Rogue waves, freight train-like wind changes, and bull-rush drift currents always had the final word. As the old timers say, "Never count your silver till you're pissing off the dock, boyo."

Jack walked back into the orange glow of the warm wheelhouse deep in thought. If all went well for the next several hours, they would be tying up at the Stonington dock around midnight. If things took a bad turn, no one would know what happened anyway. On raw nights like this, heavy weather and black water always kept the secrets.

Chapter Two - Travels

Twenty-eight hundred miles to the west in the underground SCIF facility in the Black Hills of South Dakota, Cole Mason sat with his feet up on his desk, reading the (AAR), After Action Report for a third time. A fifteen-year veteran of DARPA, based out of Virginia, he lived for his work. Any guilt he once had about what he was doing and, more importantly, who he was doing it to, had long since faded. National Security was now the mantra and just about anything that came down the pike under that heading was justified. If it walked the line of right and wrong, no one was losing sleep over any of it. All the thick, ivy-lined, moral firewalls defining the collective good in government had gone down in flames with the Nixon Administration.

Cole was relieved. The new two-year budget for the project had breezed through the congressional committee under the *Stanford Underground Research Facility* and DARPA *"black-side"* mandates, the approval providing an assurance that the breakthrough his team had been working on for the past three years could be implemented without any more pain-in-the-ass funding worries that always jeopardized the *really* important work.

The *"SCIF"*, located near Leads, South Dakota, was a massive underground maze of expansive tunnels and highly advanced labs, some a mile under the rocky soil. It had been home to most, if not all, of the Defense Department operational dark-side work since the late seventies. As an organization, DARPA was the present day main player at the facility with more than a hundred scientists and IT experts, highly classified government players who provided the grease that turned the well-worn gears for the projects at the *SCIF*.

According to the After Action Report, the designated California target had been hit and was now deep within the experiment. Things were moving quickly. Mason reached over and punched the intercom button on the phone.

"Hey, Rob, you want to come in here a minute?"

In Mason's mind, Rob Delany was a freakish hybrid transplant, one of the few Silicon Valley wiz-kids making the dangerous career leap three years ago from private sector high tech mega money to dark side government operations. The TSSCI clearance got you into the club where the Yankee White and Blue clearance grey-beards run the cubic money gig and everybody is in on the joke except the people paying the tab.

"What's up?" asked Delany, leaning into Mason's office doorway.

Mason flipped through several pages of the report before answering. "How many teams do we have on the target right now?" he asked without looking up from the papers.

"Three - two in close proximity and a bird in the air. Plus, his vehicle is wired with all possible cell and computer access," replied Delany stepping into the office. "The target is moving, heading east."

Mason flipped several more pages of the report. "Has the second target been exposed?"

Delany pulled up one of the office chairs. "Not yet. He's scheduled for a flash at 2300 EST. He's currently on a fishing boat and should be back in the harbor by then."

Mason closed the file and sat back in his chair with a deep sigh. "What's the method of delivery? And do you think the implants will stick?"

"Land-based, same as Mojave. We're pretty confident the implanted memory and the instructions will hold for months, possibly years," replied Delaney not sure what the older supervisor was looking for. He had briefed the man and the rest of the senior staff on all of the operational aspects of the mission less than twelve hours ago. "Is everything okay? From my side, I'm very encouraged so far."

Mason thought for a moment and then smiled. "We're good. There's just a lot riding on this, that's all. Keep me up-to-speed. The shot-callers do not like surprises. Oh, and let me know when the second subject is implanted."

Delany nodded. "Okay, we're on it." He tapped the edge of Mason's desk and then left the room, not wanting to linger any longer than he had to. These impromptu meetings with supervisors always held a level of career danger. The friendly banter belied a basic distrust that men of Mason's position carried. In Delany's mind, every encounter with a team senior supervisor was an exposure to uncontrolled exchange that could lead to judgment of his abilities possibly affecting any future upward mobility in the division's food chain. It was smart to tread lightly around men like Mason.

As far as the project was concerned, he was encouraged by the progress of the experiment and the predictability of the results. He felt comfortable cheerleading the mission, his operation, his idea, the basic premise first envisioned several years earlier while living in the intellectual thin air of Silicon Valley. At that time, he foresaw low-level laser use in the transference of information to the general public for the purpose of influencing the desire of goods and services in particular computers. A strong need for products, from cars to lingerie could be disseminated and programmed with his process. The eighty-year-old grandmother could find herself drawn to buying a monster truck. The raving social justice liberal could suddenly feel the urge to buy a Glock .45 caliber, long slide pistol. The morality of the ability to influence people in this way hadn't been a thought for him. Being a scientist first and foremost, the right or wrong of tagging people with a desire to buy things had been paved over by the excitement of possible process success.

His dance with the government devil started in 2015 at the Adobe Tech conference in Vegas, a week-long, geek-heavy lovefest of the latest and greatest high tech gizmos and hardware. He had presented his idea of mass-market memory product imprinting (MMMPI) using cold red and green lasers. By the time he walked off the stage following his presentation, the blue phone in the Annex building at Langley had already begun to ring. The Northern Virginia boys were paying attention and evidently had been for some time.

He had worked for years as the "go to" expert for information transference within the laser platform at Dell COM, headquartered just North of San Francisco. Six days after the conference, his chance to move past the theoretical and small lab study environment into the real world came in the form of a single phone call from a man identifying himself as a *"Mister Clearwater."* Mister Clearwater had made it very clear that he represented the best and most powerful interests of the United States Government.

Delany had quickly accepted his invitation to meet and in quick order learned that this man, who looked more like an overworked bank examiner than James Bond, had a surprising level of knowledge about the work being done at DELL COM and in particular - his work. He knew about the nanoscale semiconductor, the white laser break through, and the ability to separate the red, blue, and green laser spectrum using various temperatures and crystal settings. He knew about the new laser induced thermal cracking technology being developed in the manufacture of silicon chips. His knowledge and interest enticed him but when he spoke of doubling his personal income and increasing the level of financial support for his projects, he couldn't say "no" to "doing something good and great for America."

To be honest, Delany hadn't been impressed with the flag-waving closing, hadn't believed for a second that Clearwater or anyone else in his organization had the best interest of the country in mind. He knew that this Wilfred Brimley lookalike carrying that same steely edge came from the no-bullshit tribe of dark side intelligence sword swingers, men who smoked imported cigarettes and wore signet rings from obscure religious orders but no wedding bands. His thoughts were quickly confirmed - he represented men intrigued with heavy firepower and whatever new weapon, idea, or high tech shiny thing that could give them an edge. When they found it, they went after it hard, very hard. The Northern Virginia greybeards could smell blood in the water a thousand miles away, all the way from Vegas.

Strangely enough, it was a Walter Mitty spark of adventure that had unexpectedly flared up within his gut that had pulled him into the deep end. It had been the silver platter offer for involvement in the covert side of the equation, a real chance to look behind the curtain, something that he had never considered before. With a handshake and the exchange of business cards, the deal had been done. He had sold his stock options in DELL COM, put his house on the market, and now three years later was hip-deep in an operation that could change the world. He hadn't regretted his decision for a minute. He enjoyed the spook-central kind of atmosphere he worked in, liked the idea of carrying the level of clearance that would allow him to stand next to the President of the United States with a loaded firearm, dug the idea that he was considered a national security asset and, most importantly, savored that his work and word carried real juice in the 'behind the scenes' scientific community. In short terms - he was in his element.

***

Clay pulled off Interstate 80 into the McDonald's parking lot just three miles east of Elko, Nevada, He had stopped only for gas since leaving Mojave but now hunger, thirst, and a raging urge to piss stopped him. Stepping out of his truck, he noticed for the first time that the tie-downs on his bike had come loose, allowing the motorcycle to rest on the bedrails of the truck. Gas from the carburetor had leaked and now pooled in small iridescent puddles on the bed. He stood staring at the bike trying to clear his head from the input of equations that came with focusing on anything around him. Driving was not too bad; he was able to zone out by focusing on the road. But when he stopped and looked at something, the numbers came back in a rush.

A young man walked by carrying a grey cardboard tray of tall drinks. "Great bike! What is that, a 450?" he asked smiling.

Clay turned to the man, "Yes, YZ450, Yamaha single, weighs 245 pounds, compression ratio 12.8.1, constant mesh 5-speed transmission, seat height 38.6 inches, ground clearance 13 inches," he replied quickly, fighting the urge to expel a further listing of bike nomenclature. *What the hell was that?* he thought.

The man nodded, smiled nervously, and then walked toward his pickup, quickly digging car keys out of his front pocket. "Take care, dude," he announced, sliding in behind the wheel of his truck.

Clay watched the man drive off, knowing now that human contact, even in the mildest form was going to be a trial, especially if someone asked a question. The Messenger was right, other people, those not in the chosen few, would no longer understand him or be able to relate to how he saw the world. He had to eat, get something to drink, piss, and then get back on the road as quickly as possible. His instructions were clear and time was not something he could waste.

He had to find the team leader and be ready to leave when the ship landed. Nothing else mattered, not even the cell phone that had been ringing since he left California. He looked at the phone and recognized his wife's number. She was not here, not involved in the plan, not one of the chosen. As one of the *"unenlightened"*, she could possibly be one of the obstructionists the Messenger had warned him about. "Not important," he whispered out loud.

A sudden late afternoon gust of warm desert air blew by as anger boiled up making him twist the phone into several pieces, the plastic shards digging into his palms, drawing blood. Turning to walk into the restaurant, he tossed the remnants of the phone into the bed of the truck. By midnight he could be in Colorado, one more state closer to the team leader. Nothing was going to stop him from the mission – nothing.

Chapter Three - Road Signs

It was just after midnight when Bing, quietly thanking a god he only believed in half the time for getting home alive, pulled the last half-hitch snug securing the bow of his boat to the dock. The float into the harbor had been a nightmare of cross-currents, heavy surge, and lashing rain, turning a normally easy docking into a three-hour ordeal testing every bit of skill he had as a captain. Billy and Jack were already heading to their cars and all he wanted to do was get in his truck, go home, drink three-fingers of Jonny Walker, and sleep for twelve hours. The fishing had been crap. The little he had in the tanks would wait until morning.

Trotting across the rain-soaked parking lot, he noticed a car he hadn't seen in the area before, a newer white sedan sitting two spaces away from his pickup. *Strange*, he thought, sliding in behind the wheel of his truck, *that a car like that would be sitting on the docks at midnight.* The rain was now pounding down. The cold had given him a deep-to-the-bone chill that was making his teeth chatter as he started his truck and turned the heater up to high. He quickly rubbed his hands together as a quivering spasm ran down his back. "Shit," he whispered dropping the truck in gear. On nights like this, he felt every one of his fifty-three years.

He flicked on the high beams as he approached the large gate separating the parking lot from the access road leading to town. He knew from years of late night arrivals that no one else would likely travel the roads in this weather, except maybe old Cecil Miller, the harbor night-watchman. As he passed the gate and turned left, his lights swept across a shocking sight in the middle of the road, one that made him slam on the brakes in stunned surprise.

Not twenty feet away from the front bumper of his truck, stood a darkly dressed figure in military gear pointing what looked like an odd large-caliber rifle at his windshield. Less than a second later, a brilliant green light blinded him, jolting his head back against the headrest.

****

It was just before two-thirty AM when Harris got the call of a man standing beside his truck along the roadside in the pouring rain.

"Ah, Dispatch, who's the reporting party on this?" he asked turning northeast onto West Main Street. The rain had let up a bit as he passed the old dry-dock-yard on the left. He had never cared for water that much, never been a 'boat guy', but he did love the ocean views and leaving the Chicago PD seven years ago for the slower Maine lifestyle was the best thing he had ever done. The pay cut from big-city cop to rural county deputy had stung a bit initially but his kids were in a safe school, and his wife was a whole lot happier living near relatives that were scattered throughout the county.

He turned onto the small access road from the dock and he switched on his high beams. He flipped the switch for the bright felony stop lights on his light bar just as the tail lights from a pickup came into view. The truck was on the far shoulder of the road and appeared to have slowly coasted across, coming to rest against a low chain-link fence. He pulled his cruiser onto the grassy shoulder, parking several yards behind the truck.

"Dispatch, this looks like a minor TA. I need a 28/29 on a Maine plate -David, Adam, Ocean, 7-19. Should come back to a Ford F150 pickup."

"10-4," replied the female dispatcher. "Be advised, the RP should be there - a Mister Tolbert."

He turned on his rotating blue and red bar lights and stepped out of the vehicle just as another pickup truck eased in behind his police cruiser.

"Roger that," replied Harris into his hand-held radio. "He just pulled up."

Harris held up his hand, shielding his eyes from the truck headlights. "Are you Mister Tolbert?" he asked as the man walked up, pulling on his raincoat.

"Yep, Mark Tolbert, officer," he replied shaking hands. "I was just heading home from the Lodge, and I saw this guy standing out in the road. Damn near ran over him."

Harris nodded. "Okay, you were coming from this direction?" he asked pointing towards town as the rain started to fall again. "Where was the man standing?"

"Right about there," announced Tolbert excitedly, pointing down the street. "Standing right there, looking up like he was watching something. Scared three colors of shit out of me - standing out there in the rain and in the dark like that. Damn near ran over the crazy son-of-a-bitch.

Before Harris could reply, dispatch came back on his radio. "Ah, 17, 28/29 is clear. The vehicle is a 2007 Ford. Registered owner is a Bingemton Dushane, 1456 Almont Drive, Stonington. Are you going to need a tow on this?"

Harris keyed his mike. "Stand by, dispatch. Still trying to find out what's going on. If you have someone free, you might want to send them this way. Still not sure what I have."

"Roger, 17. Break, Sam 26, are you available to respond to 17's location?"

"Affirm, headed that way now," replied the Watch Commander. "I'm just down the road."

Harris walked over to the driver's side of the truck and was shining his flashlight into the cab just as Sergeant Pillier drove up. He rolled his window down. "Watcha got, Tim?" he asked as a distant rumble of thunder rolled out through the darkness.

"Holy shit!" shouted Tolbert pointing to the field on the other side of the fence. Harris whipped his flashlight around, illuminating a naked man, his body glistening wet from the rain, running full-out in their direction. With stunning speed, Dushane cleared the four-foot fence, landing on the road in a crouched animal-like position, his body covered with bits of grass and weeds as if he had been rolling in the wet field.

"Jesus Christ!" shouted Tolbert walking backwards towards his truck. "That's Bing Dushane! I know that guy!" his voice high and tight with fear.

"Get back in your truck, Tolbert!" shouted Harris drawing the yellow-handle taser from his duty belt. Harris kept his flashlight trained on Dushane whose darting wild eyes were swollen red as if he had been crying. Harris had seen this look before on his beat in Chicago. The crazed out-of-control stare and erratic movements were like those of someone controlled by PCP, a drug which whether smoked, snorted or injected, amplifies the heat receptors in the body frequently causing the user to take off clothes. For Harris, the primary worry was that Dushane may not even feel pain because of the adrenaline dump that comes with it. This could get bad really fast.

***

David Portia had been surprised by the phone call and even more surprised to be sitting in the same room with people he had only read about before now. He adjusted his tie and settled into the high-back leather chair trying to look as casual and relaxed as he could - like he had done this before. *They called me,* he told himself, watching more people file into the expansive meeting room. They called *me.*

"Gentlemen, take your seats, please," announced Craig Mathis to the gathering. A world-renowned Neurosurgeon and lecturer, currently the Chief of Surgery Administration and Neurosurgery at Johns Hopkins, Mathis was probably the best person in his field on the planet and an obvious choice for leadership. Portia recognized him from pictures in trade publications and news articles.

As men began to sit down around the large table, Mathis took his seat at the far end and poured himself a glass of water. Portia looked to his left and recognized several other well-respected doctors and field experts: Milton Penman, noted physiotherapist from Bethesda, known for his groundbreaking work and treatment of PTSD sufferers, to his right, Judah Ommoshant, the brilliant clinical psychologist who had been awarded the Sigmund Freud medal in Brussels last year for work in regressive memory treatment at Baylor University.

"Gentlemen," began Mathis clearing his throat, "I want to thank you all for your attendance today. It is rare that we achieve a meeting with such a vast number of exceptional folks as yourselves. For that, I thank you. Before we begin, I need to introduce our host, Mister Paul Abraham, Deputy Director of Studies and Operations at the Central Intelligence Agency."

Of the sixteen men sitting around the large conference table, Portia recognized all but two. The man Mathis had just introduced as Abraham remained seated near the head of the table. He looked to be in his late fifties, silver hair, black suit and carried the air of a high-level supervisor who did not suffer fools lightly. Portia spotted the green-faced Rolex right away. He had been looking at Rolexes for a while now, but the pay of a tenured University of Wisconsin bioengineering professor only went so far.

Abraham looked up from his leather-bound notebook, with the appearance of being annoyed, as if he had been interrupted from something far more important than this meeting. "Good morning, gentlemen," he announced flashing a quick humorless smile. I also thank you for accepting our invitation to this meeting. I first need to set some ground rules. For those of you who have worked around or with classified government information in the past, you are familiar with the anacronyms *SCIF* and *VTR*. For those who are not, *SCIF* refers to Secure Classified Information Facility. VTR refers to Vault Type Room. The rules for both are the same: no cell phones or recorders are allowed inside. No written notes are to leave the room. This conference room, gentlemen, has been designated a SCIF and a VTR. The security protocols I mentioned are therefore now in place. I know you were all asked to put your cells in the bin outside the door, but if anyone has forgotten to do so, please do it now."

"In addition, there will be no discussion or dissemination of information to coworkers, your organizations, or anyone else outside of this room for that matter. What is discussed here, stays here. This, gentlemen, is not negotiable. If anyone has a problem with any of the rules, you are free to leave. There are drivers outside that will take you back to the hotel or to the airport." He paused, making eye contact with each man sitting around the table, leaving no vagaries in his statement.

"Okay, now that we have cleared everyone in the room," he continued after a moment, "we can begin. I am going to open this meeting with a brief statement. I will then turn it back over to Doctor Mathis.". He cleared his throat and opened his notebook. "Currently the Agency is working with DARPA in a controlled study concerning *Subliminal Information Transference* via broad spectrum and the long-term effects on mental health and possible negative implications to the general public. This program has been fully funded and is in the preliminary phase of activation. Population demography is currently being selected and appropriate program monitors and support staff are being assembled as we speak. The men in this room are classified as subject matter experts and will be referred to as such. The program is designated *Ground Star,* a designation that is classified at the highest levels. I don't pick the names, gentlemen. I just make them work," he said looking up from his notes.

"Over the coming months, your input and expertise will be essential to the success of the program. Currently, this country is facing both internal and external threats that are beyond measure, threats that cannot and will not be ignored. Hard men now wait in the shadows for a chance to destroy all we believe in and our enemies are legion. It is my job, as a soldier in this war, to see that our country, a world power, has the tools and the ability to combat these challenges whenever and wherever they arise. That is our mission."

He closed his notebook and sat back in his chair. Portia sensed that Abraham had given that short speech a million times.

An awkward silence filled the room as several of the men shifted uneasily in their seats. As far as Portia knew, all the men around the table loved their country. Maybe some had a political mindset a bit left of center but their faith in what the country stood for, those core principals were without question. They had all prospered by living and working in the United States and were all probably inspired to some degree by Abraham's dedication to the cause. Yet everyone in the room had heard the words *Subliminal Information Transference*, an elegant way of phrasing *population mind control,* and it was enough to drop a cold chill on everyone in the room.

The men in attendance knew well the hidden and not so hidden frailties and weaknesses of the human mind. The very idea of the government conducting any kind of collective mind control experiment, especially on the general public, would repulse even the staunchest flag waver. This would be a hard sell.

Seeing that Abraham had no more to say, Mathis nodded and opened up his own notebook. "Thank you, Mister Abraham. Now I am going to open this meeting with an explanation, specifics as to why each of you has been invited. Please save your questions until I am finished. Hopefully, most of your initial questions will be answered as I go along. Thank you for your indulgence."

Chapter Four - Glitches

"What happened on this? When will we know the definitive cause?" Mason tossed the report on his desk and sat back in his chair. He had always known that a fatality could occur during the experiment but having one this early in the operation did not bode well for what could have been a glitch-free mission. The fifty-three-year-old Lobsterman with no history of drug abuse had been shot and killed by the police in up-state Maine, a bystander injured in the course of the incident as well. A shit-storm of inquiry had already started into why an upstanding citizen in the community free of even a traffic citation had gone berserk, having to be shot six times to stop him.

The after-action team on the ground had witnessed the shooting and were on the phone to Mason before the gun smoke had even cleared.

It was now five-thirty in the morning Dakota time, and Delany, Mason, and three other DARPA techs were seated around the large wooden conference table in a room with the three pouring over the raw data that had come in from the field as well as the After Action Report. There were indeed a lot more questions than answers.

"Guys, we have got to get this sorted out before we move forward," continued Mason. "We expect some collateral damage when we execute the full plan, but having a fatality this early in the test is unacceptable. It's only two weeks until the activation date, and this is an off-the-charts mess. I don't think I need to remind you of the importance of this program."

The last thing Delany needed was a kick-in-the-nuts motivation speech about the importance of the program. He would approach this problem like he always worked at solving and overcoming obstacles. He would get the facts, crunch the numbers, stay focused, and stay with the methodology. Having ignored Mason for a few moments, he looked up from the file he was reading.

"What was the power gain on the Maine implant? Could there have been a power fluctuation?" he addressed the tech, a recent MIT graduate who was sitting across the table thumbing through his copy.

"Ah, yeah I just read that. Here it is - 7mw, same as Mojave with a 1.5 Gb implant. The power source was the same as Mojave, a battery man-pack. Both were a target distance of twenty-five meters. It was night conditions but no reported fluctuations."

"So what was different about this shot compared to Mojave?" asked Mason working hard at controlling his anger. He hated it when the techs talked past him.

Delany thought for a moment while reading what the tech had just said. He knew he had better come up with an answer fast. There was more than just his program riding on what he said in the next thirty seconds. Judging Mason's tone, his time was just about up. "Ah, it says here that the shot was made from a standing position, twenty-eight meters away, hitting the subject through his truck windshield."

"Correct" replied the younger tech, looking at his file.

"What is the angle of inclination of a standard Ford F150 pickup truck windshield?" asked Delany, already working the numbers in his head.

"Ah, not sure what you're asking, Chief?" replied the tech, shaking his head.

Delany started scratching out some notes. "Think of light refraction studies. Glass, at a certain angle, can magnify or decrease the intensity of the beam, which means…"

"Which means," interrupted the tech, "the intensity of the shot in Maine could have been increased beyond a safe level when fired through a windshield."

"Correct," replied Delany smiling. "We need to know several things: first, the angle of the windshield, secondly, how much that inclination could increase the beam's intensity. "

"Inclination angles on domestic modern day windshields," announced the third tech looking at his laptop, "are 30, 50, and some 70 degrees. The Ford 150 has a 53-degree angle of inclination."

Delany flipped open his laptop and started punching in the numbers. Okay, I've got it here. Just give me a second. I think I know what caused the unexpected result."

The other two techs were already working the data on their laptops.

After a moment Delany spoke. "Okay, this is a preliminary workup," he said, looking up from his computer. "If we are looking at a 53-degree angle of inclination of glass with a standard thickness of 4.77 millimeters, roughly a quarter inch, then, according to these numbers, the Maine target was hit with a shot increased by .0078 percent."

The other techs continued to work the data. "I have the same thing;" replied one of the men speaking up, "point zero, zero, seven, eight percent increase in beam strength."

Mason thought for a moment. "All right, let's say, that your numbers are correct. Is that increase enough to induce uncontrollable schizophrenia in a normal person? I mean Christ-Almighty, they had to shoot the guy six times to slow him down?"

We need to check with medical on this, but given the fact that this informational light source is not your run-of-the-mill laser, I would say that negatives arising from an overly amplified shot are a real possibility."

"So, I'm going to take that as a yes?"

Delany nodded. "Yes, a strong possibility."

Mason slid the file across the table to Delany. "I'll need the concrete answers for the After Action Report within the hour, fellas. Let me know when you have it ready."

"What are your instructions on the upcoming shots already scheduled?" asked Delany, gathering his notes. "We have two more scheduled for today."

Mason sat back in his chair thinking about the question. He knew that there was no way he would be able to stop the mission, no matter how many innocent civilians got in the way. All he could do now was try to limit the body count. The five, randomly selected people to be exposed were test subjects, pawns to be studied and observed. Their behavior, good or bad, would provide invaluable data to the team.

"All right, new protocol established -no shots are to be taken through vehicle windshields or any glass for that matter. If they can't make a clear, unobstructed shot, then they are to stand down until they can. That's the new engagement policy. Is everybody clear?"

"Clear," replied Delany nodding. "I'll put the word out to the teams right away."

As the meeting ended, Mason spoke up. "Hey Rob, hold up a minute."

Delany sat back down, already knowing what was coming. The heat was on; this was the woodshed. Mason leaned forward in his chair and took off his glasses with a deep sigh. "All right, Rob here's the deal. Your reputation is not the only one riding on this. My balls are also on the table, and I do not plan on getting hit. This operation is going to happen. So whatever you have to do, whatever fires you have to light to get this program back on track, I suggest you get on it. This is not the San Francisco Google faculty lounge; this is where the sharp and necessary things happen. You understand?"

"I understand."

"I hope you do, Rob. No more fuck-ups. We need to be ahead of this."

"I understand. I feel terrible that someone got killed, I.."

"Listen, Rob," Mason interrupted. "I don't give a red-piss about some 'nobody' from bum-fuck Maine getting killed. Okay? What I do care about is the success of this program. My name is attached to it, so stop the hand-wringing about blood being spilled and get it back on track. Got it? Failure is not an option, Rob."

This was a side of Mason he had never seen before. "Yes, sir." He gathered his papers while standing to leave. The intensity of the exchange had rattled him. "I'm on it," he said, leaving the room feeling about nine-years-old. *Jesus, there is nothing like feeling threatened by someone with the capacity for carrying it out.*

As he headed toward the highly polished floor of the hallway leading to his office, he heard the high whine of self-doubt for the first time in his short government career. "Shit," he whispered. Maybe things were beginning to slip. Perhaps, despite his ability and insight, the hard edge of unintended consequences was starting to catch up.

No matter how he justified the value to the common good of National Security, a man had died in this latest trial. He hadn't pulled the trigger but knew he would have to learn to live with the raw truth that he had a responsibility for what had happened out there in the dark.

If he could have known what the future held, he would have hit the big double doors at the far end of the hall at a dead run, tossed the security badge over the fence and not stopped until reaching Bismarck. If only he had known...

Bad things were only just beginning; it was already too late to run.

***

At that very moment, a quiet army of the hardhat, orange-vested workmen were quietly working to "update" the large streetlight control boxes at every major intersection in the cities of New York, Phoenix, Denver, Los Angeles, and Saint Louis. It was a daunting task; in New York alone, all 112,470 signal lights ran through a central wireless traffic management system located in the Lindquist building in Meadowlands, New Jersey. But it was this centralization of traffic systems that worked perfectly toward the operation's success. For the planners, it had been almost too easy.

Powerful red and green crystalline lenses, each about the size of a quarter, were being installed into the detector loop of each central junction box control panel. Because the serial signal would be transmitted by satellite within the 35 to 120 second light change routine, only this tuned beam amplification would be required to generate an effective transmission. Fortunately, only one control box for every 200 light signals needed lenses. But the workers still had to ensure the height of every light, that each hung fourteen-feet from the ground, no higher than fourteen feet, four inches. It is this height that would provide optimal exposure to the beam while drivers waited and passed through the lights. Subliminal messages would repeatedly broadcast in three-second bursts on a twelve-hour cycle. Estimates were that, in a standard thirty-five second light, an individual would get at least ten deep-brain informational bursts, more than enough exposure to implant a collective memory or suggestion.

No one paid any attention to the workers. The driving public passed similar workers, similar equipment, and similar utility vehicles every day. The most extensive government population control program would begin in thirteen days, six hours and twenty-five minutes. No one saw it coming, but Operation Ground Star was hiding in plain sight - amazing.

Chapter Five - Barrel Ducks

It was almost six-thirty in the evening when Portia finally opened the door to his Marriot hotel room. The briefings had gone on all day with members breaking off into small groups after dinner to go over a series of questions given to the attendees by Abraham.

He hung his suit jacket in the small closet and kicked off his shoes, trying to remember if he had any Tylenol left in his shaving kit in the bathroom. His back hurt from sitting all day, and the headache that had been building behind his left eye was really starting to pound. He emptied his pockets, placing the change, rental car keys, and conference ID badge on the nightstand.
He stood staring at his picture on the card trying to mentally digest the last twelve hours. Never in his wildest dreams had he thought he would become a part of something like this. Government had reached an unprecedented level of technological ability and was about to change public perception of reality through this staggering capability.

His initial excitement upon receiving the invitation and then finding himself associated with some of the brightest minds had turned cold upon recognition of the focus of the program. He couldn't help but be concerned for what would happen in the next fourteen days.

As he stretched out on the bed sipping on the tiny six-dollar bottle of Johnny Walker, he thought about calling the wife but quickly reconsidered. He couldn't talk about this, couldn't express his doubts about his involvement. Hell, for all he knew, every goddamned phone was bugged. One word about this operation on a his hotel phone or his wireless would likely get several heavies to his door with full authorization to stomp his balls to mush or worse. He took another sip, feeling the burn. "Shit," he whispered to the ceiling.

A thousand miles away, a conflict of another sort was playing out.

***

"I told you to stay out of that dumpster!" shouted the man in the long white food-stained apron. "That trash and everything else in there belongs to the market. If I see you digging around in there again, I'm calling the cops."

"Yeah, go ahead and call'em, you fat son-of-a-bitch! I'm just after the cans. I ain't hurtin no one."

The man in the apron jumped down off the loading dock a lot faster than Scott thought he could have and was now within arm's reach.

"I know who you are, asshole," hissed the man grabbing the front of Scott's jacket. He jerked him close, his breath smelling like beef jerky. "I'm gonna kick the shit out of you. I've had it with you bums."

On pure survival instinct, Scott quickly whipped out a six-inch steak knife he had found in the dumpster last week. Before the man could react, he was pressing it just hard enough into the folds of the big man's chin to draw a tiny drop of blood. "Let go or I'm gonna cut you from asshole to elbow, you dipshit."

The store manager's eyes grew wide. "Okay, okay, Jesus! Relax," he replied raising his hands and backing away. "You're in deep shit now, dude," he said stepping back, pointing a finger, his eyes tight with anger. "You just threatened my life with a knife; you're going to prison, tough guy. You're in the shit now."

Scott slid the knife back into his oversized coat pocket. "Your word against mine, asshole. Ain't nobody else here," he replied, turning towards his shopping cart full of partially filled black trash bags. "I just wanted the cans, that's all." He started pushing the cart down the alley towards the street.

"I see you back here again, I'm gonna shove that knife up your ass. You got that?" shouted the clerk kicking one of the trash cans over. "I swear to God, I will mess you up! You're lucky this time."

As the shouting faded behind him, Scott flipped him off without even looking back. "Yeah, yeah," he mumbled, bumping the cart onto the sidewalk at the end of the alley. *Everyone is a badass fifty-feet away*, he thought. He checked bars and restaurant dumpsters all day with regularity but for some reason, this one seemed to be personally guarded by the fat clerk with a big mouth. No, this asshole made it a point to be a dick, like he had nothing better to do than bust someone's balls over a few goddamn cans. It was only a little past ten in the morning and if this was any indication of how the rest of the day would go, it was going to be a pisser. He threw off the interaction by spitting into the gutter and moved on.

He crossed the street and then pushed the can-filled bags further down into the shopping cart while looking in the window of the Hollister Bakery. Sometimes, the young dark-haired girl with the nose ring who worked behind the counter would give him some of the two-day-old bread and rolls that they were throwing out. If she saw him, she would usually motion for him to head to the back of the shop.

She was a nice kid and smelled good. She was always trying to get him to go to church. She would say things like 'Jesus loves you, you know' and 'God never gives up on people' as she handed him a plastic bag filled with donuts and rolls. She always made him smile standing there with her bag of bread, not having a clue how tough life could really get. A few bad breaks, a couple of bad decisions, and even she could end up sleeping in a mission, doing things for money that she would never have dreamed of before.

The mental picture of the girl living on the hard edges made him feel bad, like there are some things in life that just shouldn't get dirty, shouldn't get soiled by the piss, vomit, and stink of drunks, or touched by the greasy fingers of the perverts and scherzos he ran into on a regular basis, the shadow-people, people who had given up on life and lived in the hell of grinding deprivation and despair. No, she was clean and bright and lived in the sunshine of life. He liked to think of her always being there, always smiling, showing the kind of strength of heart it took to give a bum like himself the benefit of the doubt.

Disappointed at not seeing her inside, he pushed on past the window on his way to the recycling center three blocks away. He liked to get there before noon, before all the real losers started showing up. The bums that slept till ten, dope-sick or hung over so bad they could barely walk would scrounge a few dumpsters and then cash in what they had for a few dollars. They reminded him of zombies he had seen on that TV show - dumb, lost, and potentially lethal, people he went to great lengths to avoid.

Pushing his cart through the large chain-link gate at the recycling center, he was relieved to find the line at the can /cash window to be short. All the regulars were there - his competition. Stepping up to the scale, he dropped the three full bags on the large tray.

"How you doing today, Scott?" asked the young attendant looking at the weight readout.

"Still above ground."

The attendant chuckled and handed him a weight slip. "Good answer, bud. Here's your ticket. Karen will pay you at the window."

Shit, twelve dollars and sixty cents for a full morning's work, he thought pushing his empty cart back to the sidewalk. Working the math in his head, he came up with a dismal three-dollars-an-hour, not even minimum wage. Still, it was better than nothing. That, with the eighty-seven dollars he had saved, would become a hundred in a week, a king's ransom in this neighborhood.

Three blocks away, a plain white, newer model Ford van with darkened windows sat parked in front of the old Haskell's Flower Shop, the building now for sale. It had been a prospering community business for forty years but had closed last fall, another casualty of the internet.

"So, read me the parameters of the shot again, chief," the operator sitting behind the wheel of the van asked.

Senior Chief Dale Diamond from DEV GROUP, SEAL Team- Six leaned forward in the console's swivel chair and thumbed through several sheets of paper. He knew the answer but stalled giving it just to irritate the civilian advisor, a pretentious punk the Intel had assigned to the team.

"Indigent white male between the ages of thirty and fifty," interrupted the technical advisor from the front passenger seat. "Jesus, I thought all you tip-of-the-spear guys had a photographic memory. This was in the briefing two days ago."

Diamond laughed, "Not a bad memory, Pard, just a short one."

"Looks like we have a guy that might be a good candidate," announced the driver. "Check out the dude pushing the shopping cart about a block up."

"The guy in the long overcoat?" asked Diamond, looking through a small set of binoculars.

"Yeah. What do you think?"

The tech raised his own pair of binoculars. "About the right age, obviously homeless, probably a drunk or druggy." He looked over at the driver. "I'd say he's as good a target as we're going to find around here. Go ahead and hit him. I'll notify the chase team we've got our guy. Should be an easy one to keep track of, considering the surroundings."

The driver shifted uneasily in his seat, spitting Copenhagen into an empty water bottle. "Just like that?" he asked.

The tech lowered his binoculars, nodding. "Just like that, killer. Nobody cares who these people are."

The driver shook his head, wondering how many ranks he would lose if he throat-punched the tech. "Shit happens, dude. Any of us could end up like that," he replied deciding the twit wasn't worth the effort.

Diamond checked his response as well. The tech was just the kind of clown to bitch to superiors about a hostile work environment and Diamond had already been warned by the commander himself to get along with this man-bun ding-bat. Swallowing his words, he reached over the seat, handing the driver the small gun, a device about the size of a standard MP-five submachine gun.

"You're fully charged," he said, slapping the man on the shoulder. "First hit in broad daylight, brother. Make it count."

Outside, on the busy street, no one paid much attention to the drama unfolding in their midst. A UPS driver dashed in and out of a large brown truck as normal afternoon traffic at a fresh green light weaved through slow pedestrians still in the crosswalk. It was a normal day. The players moved through the landscape of heavy downtown activity and all the confusion that goes with it like drifting smoke - there, but not there. Barely a glance was given to the athletically built man trotting across the street carrying something wrapped in a dark green towel or the disheveled homeless man pushing the shopping cart with emptied trash bags. It was all visual white noise.

For Scott, the apparition appeared out of nowhere coming in a blinding flash of light, knocking him back as if he had been struck by a strong wind. Standing awestruck, gripping his shopping cart, his face towards the sky, he drew very little attention from those walking or driving by. The neighborhood was full of high functioning schizophrenics, homeless malcontents and now one more lunatic rambling to himself.

He may have posed a sad but normal image of mental illness to those around him, but to Scott, the scene was altogether different. He was in the presence of God, and the Almighty was telling him things, terribly wonderful things.

Chapter Six - Endings

Just before the I-44 / I-35 highway interchanges on the outskirts of Oklahoma City, Bob Dugan, of the Oklahoma Highway Patrol sat in his patrol car drinking lukewarm coffee watching the late morning traffic go by. It was just before eleven and, having skipped breakfast, lunch was on his mind.

Tacos, yeah, tacos would fit the bill. Mama Rojas down on Lake Henfer Parkway - excellent, he thought adjusting the gain on the radar unit. *If I get there before noon, the line won't be very long.*

From his position on the island under the overpass, he watched two semi-trucks speed by the posted fifty-five mile-per-hour limit, turning the radar gun numbers from white to red. *Hardly enough of an infraction to make a stop,* he thought, adjusting the volume alert tone on the unit. His violation criteria matched most of the other road dogs - ten over the limit.
He knew a real burner was bound to show up if he waited a little longer - they always did. A businessman late for a meeting, a parent late to pick up a child for a doctor's appointment, a kid not paying attention to the speed odometer – it was like shooting ducks in a barrel. It was the highly visible idiot moves, unsafe lane changes, tailgating, and speeding that led to dropping flares, rerouting traffic and the biblical paperwork that went with accidents, the part of the job he hated the most. If he could get through a shift with ten good moving-violation tickets and no accidents, it was a good day.

A motorcyclist went by in the HOV (high occupancy vehicle) lane eight over the limit and then hit a hard-brake upon spotting the marked unit. "Merry Christmas, asshole," whispered Dugan as he sipped his coffee. The reasons for the stops might be different but the words were always the same: "Really, officer? No, I couldn't be going that fast."; "Are you sure your radar gun works?"; or "How come you're stopping me and not catching the real criminals out there?"; and the one he liked the most – "I pay your salary." That one always made him smile and made the borderline ticket an absolute certainty. Whenever he encountered that little nugget of stupidity, he made sure the motorist got his money's worth.

Just as he was about to head into town, a dark blue pickup truck with California plates and a dirt-bike in the back went by at seventy-three miles an hour. "Bingo," he said, dropping his unit into drive and hitting the overhead blue lights. The bike didn't appear secure in the bed and the truck appeared to be gaining in speed. He couldn't ignore this one.

It took nearly a good mile-and-a-half pursuit before the driver finally noticed and pulled off onto the shoulder of the freeway. After parking and securing line-of-sight, he called in the plate and then stepped out of his unit. He adjusted his trooper hat, securing the backstrap from the wind of the passing cars. He hated the hat. His face was too narrow and it made him look like Barney Fife.

"Sir, roll your window down," he announced tapping the glass. The male driver rolled the window down but continued to stare straight ahead.

"Sir, I need to see your driver's license, registration, and proof of insurance, please."

"I cannot do that. I can't be late," Clay replied as he slowly rolled up his window and began dropping the truck into gear.

"Hey!" shouted Dugan hitting the window with his leather-bound ticket book, "Stop! I said stop!"

As the truck drove off, Dugan ran back to his car and quickly called it in. "County, eighteen, the vehicle on my stop just drove off, north on I-35, one male occupant. I am in pursuit."

As Clay pushed the gas pedal to the floor, a voice in the back of his mind told him to stop. This was wrong. This was not how he lived, not how he behaved. Tears streamed down his face as he fought for a small ledge of mental stability, some self-recognized familiar behavior. With the truck pushing past ninety, the mental argument cleared upon seeing the Oklahoma City limit sign flash by. He quickly wiped his eyes as the steering wheel began to vibrate in his hands. He had meant to get that front-end aligned months ago. Putting it off had been a bad decision, obvious with the worsening shimmy.

"Jesus!" he shouted as he jerked the wheel to the right, barely missing the back end of a semi's trailer that had swerved into his lane. The last thing he saw was the speedometer reading of 103 when he snapped back to the left and then dramatically back to the right, sending his truck into a blindingly-fast rollover. Clay never felt his body being ripped from the cab and ejected out the back window, nor did he feel his head strike the roadway after flying seventy-feet through the air. His death had come faster than a heartbeat.

"County, eighteen, I have a 1050 roll over!" shouted Dugan in the hand-mike as he watched the truck continue to roll and smash its way into scrap metal. "Mile-marker 7. Start rolling an ambulance." In his nine years on the road, he'd seen a hundred bad accidents. He knew no one was walking away from this one. *Christ Almighty.*

Fifteen-hundred-feet overhead and a quarter-mile back, the surveillance Bell Ranger helicopter banked right, leveled out, and headed due east. The observer kept his binoculars focused on the smoking wreck.

"Dakota control, Mongoose. Our subject has just been involved in a major TA on Highway I-35 just east of the Oklahoma City limits. Copy?"

"Roger, Mongoose. Confirming that the subject is down. Monitor local LE traffic for assessment. Find out what happened."

The observer continued to watch the grinding accident scene below through his binoculars.

"Roger, Dakota. It's confirmed. Ah, by the looks of it, our subject was ejected. That truck rolled a solid five times. I can see the body, or what's left of it, on the pavement."

There was a long pause on the other end of the radio. "Roger, Mongoose. Continue to monitor."

"Roger, Dakota." He looked at the pilot shaking his head, smiling while making a slashing motion across his throat. "Mongoose out."

***

"So, Doctor Portia, you had some concerns?" questioned Donald Gaither, a Senior Fellow at the Brookings Institute and the lead monitor of Portia's group.

This was the second day of the highly classified conference and Portia felt certain that he could not be the only one getting more uncomfortable by the hour with the subject matter of the meeting. Portia cleared his throat. "Doctor Gaither," he began, "can you reiterate just exactly where and how the feedback from this conference will be used? I am aware of the fact that this is a government population control study. My question to you, sir, is tho - Are we the architects of something that we aren't aware of? Could we learn in the future that we contributed to something that we wouldn't presently find agreeable?"

Gaither smiled, thinking for a moment. "Doctor Portia, I noticed in your question that you used the term *we*. Before I answer, I'd like to see if there are others in the group who share your concerns."

Portia sat back in his chair already regretting asking the question that had been nagging at him since last night. He knew that no one in the small group would speak up, even if some of them did have serious reservations about the project. These were accomplished men, leaders in their fields of study. They knew how the game was played, how government grants and Fellowships moved their work forward. They knew how important these high-level connections were and that rocking the boat, as it were, could end a career. He also knew that professionally he had just cut his own throat. No matter how friendly Gaither might respond, the word would be passed up the food chain that he was a nonbeliever. There would be consequences; at this level, dissension in the ranks, no matter how minor, would not be tolerated.

"Who else has concerns about the work we are doing here?" Gathier questioned, looking to the men and women seated around the large table. To Portia, who was feeling worse by the second, it sounded more like a verbal warning than a question. No one spoke.

"No one?" asked Gaither smiling. "Doctor Portia, as you can see, no one else seems to have reservations about our endeavors. Hopefully, this will give you reassurance and help you recognize the merits of what we are trying to do here. Now, if there is nothing else, we need to..."

"Doctor Gathier," interrupted Portia, "my question still stands. What is the end game for the information gathered here?" *Might as well drive a few more nails in the coffin,* he thought, taking a deep breath. This had always been his problem – he pushed the issue.

Gaither took off his glasses and leaned back in his chair, clearly irritated by the exchange. "Doctor Portia, if you are having a moral or ethical dilemma about our discussions here, I would suggest that you bring those concerns to Doctor Mathis."

Portia could feel the heat rising in his face. He was being minimized and his questions deflected with a condescending tone. It served to only motivate him more to get some answers.

"Sir, with all due respect, if we are here to construct a plan or a course of action that leads to a government population control operation, I really feel that the men and women attending this meeting need to know that from the beginning. The reason we are here has been kept somewhat vague."

"Doctor Portia, nothing is being hidden from anyone in this conference, I can assure you. I suggest that if you have deep concerns about the work being done here that you excuse yourself from any further participation. If you like, we can address your concerns offline today. Time is not a luxury we have. I will be more than happy to speak with you later."

"That would be fine," replied Portia seeing that he was not going to get satisfactory answers. Gaither held his gaze for a moment, saying more with his eyes than he could have said in an hour - he had made an enemy.

For the rest of the morning, the men in the group worked to answer the questions Abraham had presented the day before, collectively working to keep a detached clinical demeanor in the discussion. Portia knew he would be leaving after today. They may not overtly ask him to go but he knew there would be some type of suggestion that his input was no longer needed.

As he sat, quietly listening to the men speak nonchalantly about the social effects of population control and behavior manipulation, he felt more sad than angry - sad that no one else in the room seemed bothered by the discussion of a program that robbed individual freedom for the "greater good" and sad for the ease with which they spoke of the possible benefits of a program that can control an American populace and the potential effects of doing so.

Had the men seated around the large conference table forgotten the oaths of their occupations? Had each man's ethics been hanging by such a slim thread that an invitation to a high-level government meeting dripping in classified warnings and elitism was all that was needed to snap it? Is that all it took for these men, men he had thought so much of, to cross over the line? How fast the flames of moral corruption could burn a person's standards to cinders.

By seven o'clock that night, after a full day of biting his tongue, Portia sat in the far back booth of the hotel's bar and nursed a second gin and tonic while watching a group of IBM sales execs trying to out-cool each other at the bar. They all looked alike, wearing pastel polo shirts, LL Bean khaki pants, and leather loafers with no socks - the uniform of the upwardly mobile. He knew the type - fraternity guys five years out of college, neck-deep in student loan debt, mortgages, and babies on the way, all going for the brass ring. In about five years they'll be blindsided with the shocking realization that it doesn't exist. They were all shooting stars in a dead universe of corporate grooves that run deep.

Portia watched the four men and two women at the bar with a bit of melancholy. He could see himself a hundred years ago in their young faces. He took the last sip and was just about to leave when a man with silver-grey hair, appearing to be in his late fifties, walked into the bar and headed his way. The man, dressed in a dark grey suit, carried the air of a moderately successful attorney. He moved past the group and toward him.

"Doctor Portia," he announced smiling, "mind if I sit down?"

"Ah, do I know you?"

The man slid into the booth on the opposite side of the table without being invited. "Well, we've never met but I know who you are, Doctor." He raised his arm, getting the bartender's attention. "Draft beer for me. What are you drinking, Doc?" he asked, looking at Portia. "C'mon, let me buy you a beer."

"No, thanks. Nothing for me. I was just getting ready to leave. I don't need any life insurance, Bibles, or whatever else you're selling."

The man laughed, "I'm not selling anything, Doctor. I'm just here to see how you're doing."

Portia thought for a moment, trying to figure out what was going on. "Who are you? How do you know my name?"

The man handed the waitress a five dollar bill as she set the beer on the table. "No change, honey," he said smiling. She walked away, leaving the faint smell of perfume.

"I asked you a question, Sir. Who are you and how do you know my name?"

The man took a sip of his beer and sat back shaking his head, "A lot of pretty girls work here. I'll bet you that one there is about twenty-two or twenty-three and is as sweet as cotton candy," he said wistfully.

"I am not going to ask you again, I…"

"Take it easy, Doc," interrupted the man, smiling. "I'm just a messenger, a nobody, a passing shadow," he said, waving his hand for emphasis. "But you, I know all about you: tenured professor at the University of Wisconsin with a wife and two kids." The man winked. "I also know about that cute little grad student you met at the Paul Engineering symposium in Racine last summer. Boy, would that be a mess if that got out? Might unravel that tight little world you've built, huh."

Portia shifted in his seat, sweat running down his back as he tried to recall every fistfight move he had ever learned. "What do you want?" he said as his stomach began to twist.

The man took another sip. "Nothing, Doc. I was just sent here to remind you that this is a very important gathering and that you should count yourself lucky to be involved. That's all."

Portia shook his head, "Gaither sent you. Jesus, so you're the government spook sent here to put the fear of God into me about my questions in the meeting. What now? You gonna kill me? Gonna beat me up?"

The man chuckled. "Good grief, Doc. You have seen way too many Jason Bourne movies. No, I'm just here to see if you're feeling any better about being part of this process."

Portia slid out of the booth and dropped several bills on the table. "I don't know who the hell you are, buddy, but I am leaving. I…"

"Yeah, we know, Doc. You're on United flight 315 at 7:00 in the morning. It should put you home around five tomorrow afternoon, about the time Terri, your wife, gets home from work. Right? Terri is a pretty gal. You're a lucky guy."

Portia froze in mid-step. "Who the hell are you?" he asked, turning back. "Who do you work for?"

The man continued to sip his beer while looking straight ahead. "Sit down, Professor. Let's keep this civil. Okay? We both know you're not a tough guy."

Portia looked around the room and noticed that the IBM crowd had left the bar. Even the waitress was gone. He slowly sat down, feeling oddly detached from everything, like all the oxygen had suddenly been sucked out of the room.

The man finished his drink and then turned sideways in the booth with a grunt, his back against the wall. From his calm demeanor, it was obvious that he had done this before. His over-the-top self-assuredness reminded Portia of a 1930's movie gangster.

"Here's the deal. My job is to remind you," he announced pointing his finger and smiling, "that everything involved in this conference is classified and that if you feel you need to talk about this project with anyone outside of this venue, you might want to reconsider. As you can probably tell by now, we do our homework on everyone we work with," he said with a wink.

"So this is a threat then - strong arm intimidation. I'm sure you know this is highly illegal."

The man smiled slightly. "No threat, Doc, just a reminder of the sensitive nature of the project, that's all. You see, you're not the only one we have our eye on." The comment hung in the air like a bad smell.

It took a moment for Portia to understand what the man meant. "You son-of-a-bitch, you mess with my fam..."

"Sh, sh," he replied, loosening his tie. "Calm down. I am just here to remind you of your obligation of confidentiality, that's all. Your adventures in room 37 at the Hyatt are safe with me. Some things are best-kept secret, you know. That way nobody gets hurt. Are we clear there, Professor?"

Portia leaned across the table working hard at controlling his anger. "You've delivered your message. I don't appreciate being threatened. So unless you, whoever you are, have something else to say - we're done here."

The man chuckled as Portia walked off. "Have a nice flight," he announced raising the bottle of beer. "Nothing like whistling past the graveyard, huh Doc?"

Chapter Seven - Gut Check

It was 3:18 am when Delany activated spell-check a second time after putting the finishing touches on the memo that could change his life. He knew that if he went up and slipped into bed with the wife, he would just toss and turn until dawn and there was no use ruining her sleep. As he sat back staring at the lap top's screen, he recognized that this writing represented a crossroads. If he acted on it, his life would change and there was no way that that change could be anything but negative.

Just before leaving work yesterday afternoon, Mason had summoned him to his office and briefed him on the test target killed in a traffic accident just outside of Oklahoma City. Now with two deaths in the experiment, he was feeling the full emotional weight of responsibility. He had to have missed something in his calculations. In all of the computer simulations, the laser-induced stimuli had been predictable, expected to produce no amplified effect other than a pronounced subliminal idea or memory in the subject, nothing that would cause this level of mania or mental collapse. In reality, there was a glitch he simply could not ignore.

He took another sip of lukewarm Heineken from a bottle and scrolled up on the screen checking his work.

MEMO
5/23/2018
Classified/TS/SCI—YANKEE WHITE

Single copy—NOT TO BE RESUBMITTED------------------

===

TO: Deputy Director Cole Mason/ Sanford Underground Research Facility.

FROM: Robert Delany/Lead Engineer/DARPA.

Sir: I need to formally notify you of my growing concerns about the *GROUND STAR* project. I fully understand the importance of this program as it relates to the national security interests of the United States. I also greatly appreciate the opportunity and support for my work provided by the DARPA organization. With this said, I feel that the level of detrimental results that have taken place within the experiment are not acceptable and my reservations must be documented.

In good conscience, I cannot promote any program that has a potential for a pronounced lethal effect on the general population. I am convinced that more analysis and data review need to be conducted prior to the full implementation of *Phase Three* presently scheduled for initiation in seven days.

I highly recommend that all field studies using general population test subjects halt immediately. This delay is necessary for assimilation and study of the Ground Star procedures and test subjects involved with the two lethal results.

I understand that an additional test subject has been exposed to Ground Star within the last twelve hours. Because of the clearly psychotic behavior and subsequent death of two individuals previously exposed, I highly recommend that this subject is formally contacted by authorities and held in a controlled situation for observation.

I believe it is imperative that current data and calculations be reviewed and a thorough Ground Star protocol scrub performed. Good science is safe science. As the originator of this project, I urge you in the strongest terms possible to stop the exposure of the general population until we understand the recent fatalities. If these two incidents are representative of expected results, we are looking at a possible total societal collapse if we continue with the Phase Three initiation.

Continuation of the current Ground Star procedures is not in the best interests of the country. The challenges we are currently facing need to be addressed immediately.

Respectfully submitted: Robert Delany/DARPA

Nothing below this line------------------------------------

Reading the memo for the third time, he sensed the Biblical proportion shit storm that would follow his hitting the send button. Mason would call him in and blast him down to a fine powder for even suggesting that Ground Star be put on hold. As his finger hovered over the send command, he felt the weight of career suicide. A person simply did not walk away from this kind of power.

As he sat staring at the screen, he was suddenly hit with a thought - a jolting realization that had not come to mind before this moment. Maybe his calculations were not wrong. Maybe something else had been added to the mix that was literally driving exposed people to insanity. It had not even occurred to him until now that someone could be tampering with the arrays, amplifying the impute, and changing the message. It would explain the failures but it was a sobering thought that for someone to actually change the program it would have to be a person he trusted, someone who had worked by his side every day for the last two years.

The big wall clock in the hall softly chimed on the half hour. *My God,* he thought, looking at his watch -*3:30 am. The operation is set for rollout in seven days.* If the work wasn't subverted, the world as he knew it would end on that seventh day. He took a deep breath as a cold shiver ran down his back. In a moment of absolute clarity, all doubts of what he needed to do vanished.

He pushed the send button and sat back with a sigh, suddenly exhausted. Running his hands through his hair, he knew that whatever fallout that would come from his memo would most likely hit within the next three hours. He took the last swallow of the warm beer, the seventh-day Biblical reference not lost on him. As he slowly made his way down the darkened hallway to bed, he knew that he could possibly save the world with his efforts and cut his own throat in the process. Slipping into bed beside his sleeping wife, he had no illusions of success in stopping anything, only the growing deep-seated dread that he was already too late. Whatever the outcome, his life would change. No matter which path he followed, his life could come to a swift and bloody end. Resigned to his fate, he fell asleep.

Shifting the universe always demanded a price from gods and mortals alike – always.

***

Ninety-three dollars and sixty-four cents. That will have to be enough, Scott thought, stuffing the small Ziploc bag of money into his coat pocket. It was two-thirty in the afternoon. Having walked through the bad part of North Saint Louis without problems earlier in the day, walking across EADS bridge should be a snap.

It felt strange to not have the shopping cart; it had tied him to daily survival for the last four years. Now, everything he owned was tied up and in an old $3 rucksack purchased at Goodwill. It was three dollars he could ill afford, but the Angel had said it would be okay. That and whatever else he needed to do to get to the team leader would be watched over and protected by the Angel. He smiled at the feeling of assuredness in his heart, something he had never felt before. This overwhelming sense that his journey had been divinely ordered was beyond special.

A cold gust of wind rose up from the wide brown expanse of the river sixty-feet below. Even from this height, he could see that the current was moving at a good clip. He tried to remember when he had last been this close to the Mississippi. He had seen St. Louis Arch in the sky-line almost every day, yet not having walked more than a mile from the shelter over the last four years, the river, a visual part of the city's white noise, was unfamiliar to him. He thought of what he was leaving behind.

He had skipped out on a week's rent at the shelter, settling the debt in his mind with the things he left behind: an ancient microwave, a toaster, and a blue plastic milk crate full of old candles. He had dug the scented candles from dumpsters because they reminded him of his life before. The scent of Christmas pine and apple pies recalled a time when he wore clean clothes every day, when the terror of life on the street belonged to other people. He had had a real job back then, a decent roof over his head, hot showers that weren't at the end of a waiting line, and food that came from his own refrigerator.

He wiped dust from his eyes, dust kicked up by a semi that had rolled by. He kept an even pace of movement across the bridge while continuing to lament soft memories of a time when he wore a plastic badge with his name on it and carried a lunch to work.

He smiled at the memory of the meals she had packed for him: sandwiches made the way he liked them, chips in their own separate container and a cold can of coke wrapped in tin foil to keep it cold. Erin had been the emotional glue in his life, and he loved her for this and all the other little things she did for him.

It had been a terrible day five years ago in September when it had all fallen apart. He winced at the memory of the two State police officers who had shown up at his work that day. He recalled their grim faces as they walked towards him, their keys jingling as they approached. He pulled his collar tight against the wind now as he remembered their words, "Your wife and daughter were fatally injured today." At that moment his hearing had shut down and his knees had buckled.

He later learned that she had more than likely not even seen the truck that killed her. Even though it had taken emergency crews an hour to cut her and his two-year-old daughter out of the car, he had been assured that their lives had ended at impact. They hadn't suffered the emotional loss that he was left to endure.

He shook his head and wiped away a tear, willfully focusing on the comfort that had come with the Angel's appearance. In an instant, the Angel had healed him, giving him purpose - a higher calling. Things were set right now. The booze needed to make the pain go away over the last five years would never again drive him into the ground. He hadn't had a drink for over two days now, not even once having a craving. It was a miracle, one that he would never forget.

He spotted the big green and white *Welcome to Illinois, The Land of Lincoln* sign hanging over the last part of the bridge. With each step, he felt lighter - cleaner. He was breaking away from the dirt, despair, and heartache associated with the city and moving into a different existence, one that held a spectacular promise. All he had to do was get there. The knowledge that the amazing promise would be revealed when he reached his destination made him feel alive for the first time since Erin's death.

To the men in the unmarked white van parked a block away, the disheveled bearded guy walking past carrying the faded orange rucksack was nothing more than a target of surveillance, a nameless person carrying no more importance than a hundred other human targets they had been assigned to over the years.

For them, life now revolved around the speed and distance covered by the walker. Finding a place to piss, locating decent fast food, and calling in his progress made up the itinerary.

Chapter Eight: Revelations

"You know, I have found over the course of my career that even some of the smartest men have made bad decisions, doing dumb things that changed the trajectory of their lives forever." Mason sat back in his chair letting the statement hang in the air. Mason had been waiting when Delany had arrived in the office a little after seven am.

Taking a deep breath, Delany sat down opposite Mason's desk, the sweat already running down his back. "I stand by the memo. I think we need to reevaluate our data, I think…"

"All right, let me stop you right there," interrupted Mason angrily. "I just don't believe you appreciate the importance of the work we do here, Robert. I have covered this ground with you before. Do you really think your misguided apprehension concerning this project will have any effect on its release? Is that your assumption? "

Delany was not about to be pushed around; he had to express his suspicions. "I believe my original work on this program has been tampered with. I need to go back over all the data. I think there's a major problem."

Mason sat back in his chair, his expression flat. "Here's what we are going to do," he replied, his tone measured as if fighting for control. "As of this morning, you are officially on terminal leave."

"Terminal leave? What does that mean?"

Mason thought for a moment. "I can't have someone on my team who cannot be trusted to carry out the critical mandates of this time sensitive operation. Go home. Discussion is over."

"You can't be serious? This is just as much my project as it is yours. I...."

"That's enough, Robert," interrupted Mason. "You're done. Go home. I am deeming you unfit, pending a review. I am tired of you trying to subvert this program. It stops today."

Delany shook his head, stunned by what he was hearing. He knew Mason would be upset by the memo but this seemed over-the-top. "What is going on here? Subvert the project? For God's sake, I am the lead on this project. Something is wrong and we need to correct it before this goes online. I have a moral obligation to get this right."

Mason slowly stood up from behind his desk. "I suggest you do what you've been told, Robert. I've given you a direct order. It would be in your best interest to follow it. I am not concerned about your moral obligation."

"So, you are actually removing me from the program? I am no longer part of what is going on here? Is that it?"

Mason nodded. "That is exactly what I'm telling you, Robert. Your services are no longer needed. Go home. Don't make this any harder than it already is. I'll contact you later this week."

Delany knew his career was over. There would be no coming back from this confrontation. He shook his head and laid the copy of the memo on Mason's desk. "God help us," he whispered.

He stood and slowly left the office, closing the door behind him. *Jesus,* he thought, heading down the long hallway. *What just happened?* As he entered the facility parking lot under an early morning sunshine, he could smell bridges burning.

***

Scott left a tall stand of trees just off the highway a little before dawn after having a decent night's sleep and now stood studying the McDonald's menu sign on his 2nd day of the journey, carefully calculating the price of a meal. He had a long way to go, and he needed to stretch the ninety dollars in his pocket as far as he could.

It had been years since he had been in a fast food place. His meals at the shelter had been supplemented with food found in the dumpsters of restaurants around the city, the scavenging all a part of his normal routine. As he stepped up to the counter to give the older woman his order, a group of noisy teenagers walked into the building and got in line behind him.

This was a treat, one he could ill afford, but he was hungry. For a moment, he almost felt like a normal person. A melancholy memory of standing in line with his daughter waiting for a Happy Meal a lifetime ago hit him hard in the chest.

Shaking the images from his mind, he focused on the brightly lit menu board. "Ah, I would like an egg McMuffin, a large coffee, and two hash browns. And ma'am, do you have any burnt things you're going to throw away? I'll take em if you've got em."

The woman looked up from the cash register. "Ah, I don't believe we have anything like that, sir. Sorry."

"That's fine," replied Scott, suddenly feeling self-conscious for asking. He could only imagine how he looked to the woman in his less-than-clean clothes and disheveled hair. "How much do I owe you, ma'am?" he asked pulling the zip lock bag from his coat suddenly noticing how dirty his hands were. Embarrassed, he had to fight the urge to just walk away.

The woman punched in the order. "That will be three dollars and forty-six cents. Would you like cream and sugar in your coffee?"

Scott thought for a moment. "Is that extra?"

Several of the teenagers snickered. "Loser," coughed one of the boys into his hand just loud enough to be heard.

The woman smiled sadly. "No, sir. It comes with your order. How much would you like?"

"Nice wallet, dude," laughed one of the boys behind him as Scott carefully pulled out the crumpled bills and change.

Just as he was about to hand the woman the money, a large bearded man in heavy work clothes wearing a Mack Trucks baseball cap suddenly appeared beside him. "I got this, pard," he said handing the woman a twenty.

Scott looked at the man surprised. No one had ever stepped up and paid for anything for him - ever. "I can pay my way," replied Scott to the stranger.

The man looked over and smiled. "I know you can, pard. Ma'am, I'll take a large coffee - black and one of those blueberry muffins." He looked at the group of teenagers. "You dipshits got anything else to say?" He spoke with an unmistakable menace in his voice. "I'm sure we all want to hear it?" No one said a word. Even the other patrons became quiet.

"Ass holes," he mumbled as the woman quickly went about filling the order. "I've been on the road too, brother. Just paying back what other folks have done for me," he said before nodding a thank you to the woman as she gave him his coffee, muffin, and change. "Hang in there, guy." He gave a thumb's up and brushed past the group of teenagers who quietly stepped aside and was out the door before Scott could thank him.

The woman handed Scott a bag after dropping in two additional muffins with the rest of the food. "I'm pretty sure those were burnt," she said smiling. "You have a good day, sir."

***

Four hundred miles to the south, Portia was about to ease back into his academic role after attending the conference in DC. His life was normally a comfortable one: a tenured professor at the University of Wisconsin, family man, responsible, a solid pillar of the local academic community complete with all the trappings of successful middle America family life - a three bedroom house in an upscale neighborhood, a pretty wife devoted to her children and husband, and a growing respectable 401K. He had all the boxes checked of stability. But now, as he drove through the early morning commuting traffic, a thick pervasive dread had taken hold.

A fear was distracting him at a level, unlike anything he had experienced before. Even his wife had noticed it in his loss of appetite for food and sex and in his inability to rest, leaving him tossing and turning throughout the night.

He found himself checking the rear-view mirror incessantly as he drove toward work. He had no idea what he was looking for. He just couldn't shake the feeling that he was being watched, monitored.

Pulling into the faculty parking lot on the west side of the campus, he knew he would have to somehow confront the fear, finish whatever had been started when he accepted the invitation to go to Washington DC. Living this way, feeling a threat but not knowing for sure, was far worse than confronting the source of his anxiety.

The busy familiar atmosphere of university life closed in around him as he parked in his normal spot.

He collected his papers and briefcase, in his mind rehearsing what he was going to say to staff when the inevitable questions about the conference came. Of course, he would lie, saying that the trip had been a monumental bore, that the only thing he got out of going was a few Washington DC souvenirs and outrageous charges from the hotel mini bar.

He would have to keep it together, being careful to not let anyone see how rattled he really was by the trip. With the warning from the agent at the restaurant still ringing in his ears, there was no way he could explain what the meeting had really been about.

As he pushed his way through the large glass doors of the building, he caught his reflection. *Smile*, he whispered to himself, *smile*. Taking a deep breath, he stepped up to the chest-high reception counter. "Morning, Mary," he said cheerfully to the heavyset woman busily typing away on her computer.

She looked up and smiled. "Ah, you're back. How was the conference?"

"It was okay, I guess. Nice to see the city. Do I have any mail?"

She turned in her chair. "Ah, yes. As a matter of fact. Fed Ex dropped this off for you yesterday afternoon." She handed him an envelope.

He immediately checked the postmark and recognized the DC zip code. "Thank you, Ma'am. I'll be in my office." He nodded and smiled in a way that he hoped was normal and headed down the hall. He already knew what was in the envelope. Inside his office, he stacked his briefcase and papers on the desk and, with a deep breath, peeled open the seal. Inside was a single sheet of paper and a high resolution black and white photograph.

His heart pounded an extra two beats as he looked at the photo of the grad student he had the brief fling with last summer. The picture appeared to be recent which was even more alarming; it had almost been a year and a half since he had seen her. He stuffed the picture back in the envelope and read the letter.

Greetings Professor Portia,

Just a short note from a friend to remind you that, as responsible professionals, we must honor our commitments. People – friends, colleagues, wives, people we care about - are depending on us to do the right thing. I know I can count on your continued support.

Regards to you and your beautiful family at 2356 Hollings Hill Drive. You're a lucky man, Professor.

Stay well, sir,
A. Smith

A sick feeling overcame him as he slowly sat down behind his desk to reread the note. He knew that his life would never be the same; a new sharp-edged normal had arrived, and there wasn't a thing on God's green earth he could do about it. "Son-of-a-bitch," he whispered.

Chapter Nine - Visions

For Delany, the more he thought about it, the more impossible it seemed to explain to his wife what had happened at work. They had sold everything to get to South Dakota so he could take this government job. They had left friends behind, long-term social circles back in California, totally changing their lives. Even though the move had put his wife closer to her family, she would not take this lightly. Tears would be shed and resentment would take root no matter how many words of contrition accompanied the news.

Two years ago, he had been a rising star in the tech world, accepted in the thin-air of forward-thinkers and industry movers, his position as the golden boy secured. Now sitting in his car in front of Dunkin Donuts, he felt like just another government employee waiting for the pink slip, the ticket for a much dimmer phase of life.

For the last two days, he had been living a lie, getting up early, having his coffee and peanut butter toast at the kitchen counter, packing a lunch, and then getting out the door by 7:30. He had spent the working hours driving around town, sitting in the library, and drinking coffee in empty parking lots, all the while trying to think of what to do next.

He had called the office at least thirty times, leaving messages with no response. He had driven back to the complex only to find that his badge and proximity card no longer worked at the access gate. He had been cut off - banished. In his entire adult working life, he had never experienced this kind of professional isolation. Even as a teenager he had run with the popular crowds, driving the right kind of car, wearing the right type of clothes, and dating the pretty girls. In adulthood, his intellect and family connections kept him in the protected clicks, insulating him from low paying entry jobs and limited options. Carrying the relaxed air of the well-heeled, he always had money and opportunity. Now, for the first time in his life, he was on the outside looking in, a feeling that had begun to make him feel physically ill.

He sat in the parking lot, staring out his truck's rain-flecked windshield, quietly drinking the lukewarm coffee and mindlessly eating the overly sweet maple bar. He was trying to come up with the courage to call his wife and tell her everything that had happened. It was just before noon and, finally a plan began to take shape.

"Bullshit," he whispered, angrily tossing the half-eaten pastry into the paper sack. *Enough of this victim shit,* he thought, starting the truck. *Time to go on the offense. Getting slammed for wrongdoing was one thing; getting ripped on the job for just being cautious was another.*

The tools, information, and connections to help his cause were at hand. He was not about to lay down and lose everything he had worked for his whole life. He knew people, powerful people who would help him.

He slowly began backing out of the parking spot. He didn't see the heavyset bearded man until he was suddenly standing four feet from his side window. For a split second, Delany thought he saw a large weapon in the man's hands. Trying to process what he was seeing, his body locked up from an over-powering, involuntary blast of adrenaline as he fumbled with the gearshift. A heartbeat later, a blinding light slammed into his eyes, jolting his head back.

Dazed and disoriented, he watched as an angel slowly appeared from a hazy golden light. Time suspended, spatial references became skewed, and the only sound was that of his own breathing. As the angel drifted closer, Delany desperately fought for some rational mental edge to stand on, some reasonable explanation for what he was seeing. He was falling, drifting in the blinding light, his mind a whirl with tearful questions and awe. Rational thought, like shiny silver coins, dropped in dark water, flipped into the abyss far below, replaced by an absolute focus of attention on the angel.

The angel did not speak, yet Delany heard the voice as clear as thunder as the apparition drifted even closer. "You are chosen," announced the voice in a tone of compassionate control. "You need to travel to the east."

"Are, are you God?" whispered Delany, tears streaming down his face.

The angel shimmered and then drew back, its form hovering in midair. "Find the holder of the manifesto," commanded the voice. "He, along with the rest are waiting for you there. I am the Messenger."

For a fleeting second, a razor-thin jolt of skepticism flashed through his consciousness. There was something off about the vision; the interaction seemed oddly impersonal, like a family member's voice on an answering machine - familiar, human, yet noncognitive. "Why was I chosen?" he asked fighting the overpowering urge to let go, to give in to the vision.

The angel drew closer, the intensity nearly blinding. "Stonington is where they are gathering. They are waiting for you there. Only the chosen are called. I am Uriel. I am the Messenger."

***

Standing in the rain beside the highway was nothing new for Scott. He had dropped his fear of hitchhiking years ago. If a lunatic wanted to kill him, so be it; they would be doing him a favor. On the streets, he had the reputation of having brass balls, of being a real hardass. In reality, he was just suicidal, a broken-soul, tough guy who lacked the courage to take himself out of the game. The crazy brave are often mislabeled.

But things had changed. The angel had removed the dark shroud of booze and self-loathing from his mind, giving him the heart-racing jolt of hope, something he had not had in years.

It was just before noon when an eighteen-wheeler pulled to a stop and picked him up on the access road. Grateful to be out of the downpour, Scott crawled up into the cab, stuffing his soaked backpack under his feet as the driver dropped the truck in gear.

"Name's Bob Rich. What's your name?" shouted the driver above the truck engine noise as he merged onto the freeway.

"Scott," he replied nodding. "Thanks for the ride."

The driver upshifted. "Well we're not supposed to pick up hitchhikers, but you looked like you were about to drown out there. Sometimes, the wrong thing to do is the right thing. That's my motto. Where you from?"

Scott thought for a moment, "Saint Louis, and not the good part either." He hadn't meant it as a joke, more of a declaration.

Rich laughed while checking his side mirrors. "Well, I've been just about everywhere in the last 24 years and the only thing I like about Saint Louis is the barbecue. I like Pappy's Smoke House, down on Olive street. You ever been there? Best ribs ever."

Scott pondered the question trying to figure out a way of answering without getting thrown out of the truck. The only thing he ever did in Saint Louis was drink himself sick, collect cans, and live in a homeless shelter, not a whole lot on which to hang a decent conversation. He looked down at the small red and white cooler that had the word *IGLOO* written on top. "You wouldn't happen to have any of those ribs in that box would ya?"

Rich laughed. "Nope. Sorry, pard. But there is half of a turkey and ham sandwich from Subway in there if you want it." Still keeping his eyes on the road, he reached down and slid the box over. "Go ahead; you look like you could use something to eat."

"You sure?" asked Scott, feeling as though his stomach was trying to gnaw a hole to the backbone.

"Hell yeah, my friend. Wife wants me to lose this beer gut anyway. Go ahead. There's an extra Doctor Pepper in there. Still might be cold. Help yourself. I've got a bunch more in the sleeper fridge in the back."

Outside, the rain continued to pound down on the windshield of the truck, the wipers barely keeping up with the flow. As he ate, Scott let the older man talk. Listening to his stories about icy roads, bad truck crashes, and good places to eat on the road required minimal responses. For Scott, Rich's incessant talking was white noise, oddly comforting in its tone and pace. As he watched the landscape roll by outside, the vision of the angel was just as clear in his mind as it was the day it first appeared, the emotional mandate to go east stronger than ever.

But that was a lie. The feeling of assuredness following the vision about what he was supposed to do had changed. A perceptible edge of doubt had begun to grow about the reality of what he was doing. *People don't see visions,* he thought, drinking down the last bit of Doctor Pepper, *at least not sane ones.* Maybe the alcohol abuse had reached a level that prompted hallucinations. Maybe his brain was now so eaten up by the lifestyle of living on the edge, that he was seeing and reacting to apparitions of his own making.

"Hey, Bob," he interrupted, "You ever heard of a town called Stonington, somewhere on the East Coast?"

Rich thought for a moment. "As a matter a fact, I have. It's a small fishing town a few miles from Brunswick, Maine. Made some runs up that way a couple of years ago. Oysters mainly. Nice place. People talk funny. Hey, that reminds me of a story I…"

"So, it's a real place?" interrupted Scott again.

Rich nodded. "Yeah, sure. Not very big though; couple thousand people tops. Why you ask?"

Scott stuffed the empty sandwich wrapper and soda can into the small trash bag hanging from the dash. "I guess that's where I'm headed, Bob."

An eighth of a mile behind Rich's truck, the unmarked white van with darkened windows kept an even pace, a pace just back far enough to not raise suspicion but close enough to stay in sight. The men inside had watched and mused at Scott standing in the rain for hours before being picked up by the truck, even laughed about the idea of giving him a ride themselves.

"We're going to need gas pretty soon," announced the driver checking the gas gauge.

The team leader, sitting in the passenger seat, looked up from his laptop. "That truck can go a lot farther then we can before filling up. We need to stop him for a bit."

The SEAL in the back shifted in his seat, "You have any ideas?"

The civilian team leader smiled as he typed in an entry on his computer. "Yeah, I just patched into the Indiana State Police mainframe reporting this truck stolen. Also patched in a witness sighting at the mile marker we just passed."

"That's a pretty shitty thing to do," replied the SEAL shaking his head. "That's gonna fuck up that guy's whole day when the cops do the felony stop."

The team leader turned in his seat. "Not my problem, dude. Who gives a shit about some nobody, Joe Dirt truck driver?"

The van driver looked over at the civilian. "Hey asshole, my old man was a truck driver. Jesus, I'm really tired of your shit. Are you just looking to get your ass kicked, bud?"

The civilian laughed. "Wow. You always threaten people you work with, tough guy? I wonder what your boss would say about that."

The driver took out his cell phone and slammed it on the dashboard. "Here ya go, motherfucker. He's on speed dial. Go for it."

The civilian grabbed the phone off the dash. "You don't think I would do it, do you? There are a hundred guys within Special Operations that would give their left nut to be on this detail. You have no idea how fast your career warning light is now blinking, Einstein."

The driver was about to reply when a duel flatbed truck bound for the new Mercy Hospital in Indianapolis carrying four twenty-eight foot steel beams swerved into traffic from the on-ramp. No one saw the small red flags wired to the ends of the overhang, flags that punched through the windshield and the driver in a blinding spray of shattered glass, blood, and bone. The driver of the flatbed, feeling the impact, locked the trailer airbrakes which only drove the heavy steel beams further through the van and out the back doors, taking the Seal team leader's left arm and most of the shoulder with it.

It took a solid four hours for the State Police to remove the dead, transport the only survivor, a civilian government employee who was unconscious and in critical condition, fire-hose the blood off the street, and clear the highway.

A dispute had ensued between the Highway Patrol officers working the accident and a four-man Federal unit who showed up within minutes of the crash to start removing equipment from the wreckage. After a heated face-to-face with the officers at the scene and several phone calls, the Feds were grudgingly allowed to remove whatever they wanted including the identification and handguns the military victims had been carrying. The accident report and photos were quickly classified and confiscated and sealed under the National Security protocol. Nothing was being left to chance - nothing.

Chapter Ten - Lock and Load

Mason knew the timeline for both operations was going to be moved up. The body count was growing, trending pretty much the way the operational matrix said it would, an acceptable problem for those in power. Collateral damage was just the price of doing business.

Non-believers, general malcontents, and individuals with congressional oversight who built careers poking holes in the black side of things were dealt with in the fashion required. The Potomac River was shallow and gave up its dead. More than once a polished sculling boat on an early morning run had hit the corpse of someone who got too close to the blue flame. In some way sooner or later everyone in town would get the message.

In DC, positions of influence were awarded for saying and doing what the shot callers expected. The voters got you in the door, but the real brokers of power kept you there. By design, platforms and controversies such as NAFTA agreements, trade wars, abortion rights, and gun control kept the public, pundits, and media battling one another. But whatever hot-button issue was currently debated on the national stage was never the real issue. The real issues were decided on the other side of the curtain.

For the boys at the Skull and Bones charter room, the Bohemian club, or the meat eaters and ring knockers on K street, the labels of Democrat and Republican were nothing more than different-colored jerseys for people playing in the same high stakes game. The fix was already in, and everyone knew it.

Power and population control were the real prizes and had been for decades. Everyone involved at the top could care less than a red piss if some GS 14 or GS 15 took it in the neck. Each was a replaceable part in a machine that had to be kept running. Elections and Presidents came and went and social agendas changed with the tide, but the real power of the entrenched ruling class in the United States never loosened its iron grip on the reins of power. Even the Supreme Court with its sweeping rulings creating constitutional mandates didn't intrude on the primary hidden objectives. The "collective good' argument for the general populace was always good enough to move the agenda forward as long as their small world of fast food, Facebook, Instagram, and data streaming was not threatened. If the status quo didn't appear to be shaken, there was no need for the American public to learn about the country's quiet yet incredibly powerful ruling class.

Mason sat back in his chair and read the final test headings that would be released starting two days from now. Google, Facebook, and every other social media giant had been briefed on what to look for and relay back through classified channels. The Akashic Records and the Drake Equation, both complex subjects and not well known by the general population, would be the first microburst street-light transmissions sent throughout the Midwest and parts of New York City. If the messages were absorbed in the collective consciousness of the population, they would show up on the Internet and social media trends almost immediately. Demographics would be made available in real time on a broad-based level, a wet dream for the data crunchers.

For those in power, the advancements in computer and Internet technology had become the new weapons used with stunning effect. The populace was gleefully buying the newest and best toys that seemed to come out every year, waiting in lines and paying thousands for gadgets that transmitted personal data on a massive scale, unwittingly providing the keys for their collective electronic prison. It was almost too easy.

As far as operational housecleaning went, Mason's order to hit Delany with the amplified array had been an easy decision. He wouldn't miss the condescending manner the Silicon valley wiz-kid had worked with the other team members or the elite intellectual status Delany wore like a badge. More subjects had been needed to provide invaluable information about how the transmission affected a person. Delany was just as good a test subject as any.

***

After receiving the photograph and the veiled threat, Portia's days had been haunted by a pervasive, barely manageable dread. For the first time in his life, he was afraid of being exposed as an adulterer, someone not trusted to keep his hands off the endless parade of eager grad students. It was the kind of bad rap that stuck to a person for life, deserved or not. He had seen the accusation of bad behavior take down more than one of his colleagues in the recent past and had sworn that it would never happen to him.

Craig Heppner, the most recent casualty, had been a respected physics professor caught by the police balls deep in one of the grad students in the back seat of his wife's car last year in Bessemer Park. After a furious father's complaints led to a plethora of bad press from the local rags, the university had used the contract morality clause to take him down. He lost everything - family, possessions, tenure -18 years down in flames.

The phrase "consenting adults" meant nothing nowadays. Millennial females, liberal fire-breathers looking for a scalp and a reason to be offended carried out the hunt for the white-male sexual predator. "Sexual predator" was just the latest label, a cancerous little PC nugget festering in the social justice cabal well distanced from the Clinton Lewinsky nonsense.

Heppner's fate haunted him. He went from a 2800 square foot home on Crestwood Drive with a boat, a Lexus, and all the other clean and shiny trappings of an upper-middle-class suburbanite to a two-bedroom apartment downtown and a substitute teaching gig at the community college. Last time Portia had seen him, the man had lost thirty pounds, grown a half-ass beard, and wore a blue-bead earring in his left ear - not a good look for a fifty-five-year-old man. *Jesus,* he thought, heading to his car, *that could be my future.*

The sudden heavy jolt of fear made him weak in the knees as he slid in behind the wheel of his car. He couldn't stop thinking that it could all begin to unravel tomorrow. This could be the last time he would head home from a long day as a respected educator. A meaningless fling could result in a duck walk out of the only job he loved. It was amazing on how thin a thread our lives hung.

He dropped the car in reverse and was about to back out when a stout man in a dark suit appeared at his window. The man tapped on the glass. "Professor, can you roll the window down?" Before Portia could stop himself and against his better judgment, he pushed the button to lower the window. "Can I help you?"

The man smiled without humor. "Well, not really, my friend." He raised a short-barreled weapon from under his suit jacket and fired a blinding beam of light into Portia's eyes. Another loose end taken care of.

***

Outside of Indianapolis, just before interstate 74 turned into interstate 465, Rich pulled into the expansive parking lot of the Pilot fueling station and slowly backed in between two eighteen-wheelers in a long row of trucks parked across from the restaurant. Scott pulled his backpack off the seat after stepping out of the cab as Rich walked around the front of the truck. "They serve a pretty good chicken-fried steak here," he announced smiling.

Scott thought for a moment. "Naw, I better not. I'm kinda short on funds. I think I'll just hit that McDonald's over there on the way out."

Rich took off his baseball cap and wiped his brow. "Damn, partner, I can help you out there. My treat. Jesus, God knows I've been down on my luck a time or two."

Scott extended his hand and smiled. "You've done enough, my friend. Thank you for the offer and the ride, but I do want to be moving on."

Rich shook his hand. "Well, all right then. You take care of yourself there, pard."

Scott nodded and pulled the backpack on. "Okay. Thanks again." Rich patted him on the shoulder as he walked by.

As he walked across the expansive truck yard parking lot, Scott let the memory of another time in a similar place drift through his thoughts. It was the first vacation he had taken with Erin when they had driven up to Idaho to visit Erin's Aunt Terri, a woman who had practically raised her through the countless summers she spent growing up there.

They had stopped at the Flying J Travel Plaza, just outside of McCamdan, Idaho, for lunch and gas. The baby was less than a year old, and he smiled remembering how Erin carried her around in one of those cloth sarongs, a Pier One South American import, sported by all the yuppie moms at the time. She had liked the closeness of the baby to her heart and the functionality of making it easier to breastfeed in public areas - nothing going on in here, just a kid wrapped in a blanket.

She was such a great mom, he thought, watching several more trucks pull in from the highway. She had deserved so much more, deserved to see her daughter grow up, to see her go to school, go to dance-class, go to high school, and a million other events in the life a young woman.

The shaded memory of that stilted walk through the hospital and into the emergency room that terrible day, seeing them both freshly dead laid out on the blood-stained sheets on separate gurneys was an image that had burned deep into his brain. It had angered him to see the separation of the two. Why couldn't they lay his little girl next to her mother? Was that too god-damned much to ask?

As he pushed the memory away, he stepped inside the brightly-lit McDonalds and brushed away the tears that came every time he thought about his little girl alone on that gurney, the pain and horror of that day always within easy reach of his memory.

He didn't want to eat. He just needed a quiet place to sit down to think and collect himself. The vision of the angel was just as real as it had always been but the memory of the angel's voice was fading, like someone talking in a long dark tunnel - there but not there.

He slid into one of the far booths with his back to the never-ending procession of kids, parents, and elderly getting a fast-food fix. At that moment, as he stared at his reflection in the window, he never felt more alone, more detached from the world. He was a ghost, an anchorless soul adrift in a reality where everything and everyone except him moved at the speed of light. He smiled sadly at his reflection, knowing that no matter what he did, how he prayed, or how much he tried to drink it all away, he would never get over the loss of the only woman he truly loved. Some wounds were just too deep to heal. All of his hopes and dreams had ended in that overly-lit emergency room.

His only task in life now was to keep moving east, get to a town he had never heard of, and try to make some sense of it all. As he pulled himself out of the booth, he remembered something one of his AA sponsors had said back at the mission about faith.

The man, a recovering alcoholic himself, had pulled him aside after one of the meetings and, with the sincerity of an executioner, said that for any man, it was impossible to please God without faith. Faith was believing in what you could not see or hear but believed nonetheless.

For Scott, as he stepped outside in the late afternoon sunshine, faith was nothing more than a five letter word; it meant nothing. He wasn't heading to Stonington on faith; he was going there because he had no other place to go, and if he didn't keep moving, he might very well find a lethal way to stop the pain. Faith was a luxury he could no longer afford. For others, it was an emotional ledge to stand on when facing the abyss. Hell, he had jumped off that ledge years ago. He had been falling in the dark ever since.

Chapter Eleven – Green Light

The thing Mason liked most about the conference calls in the SCIF was the candidness and detail oriented discussion, unlike the phone conversations with the upper echelons during the week where subjects were intentionally vague.

"So what is the collateral damage with the amplified array exposure? My understanding is that it is high."

Mason sat back in his chair and opened the file on the table. The question had come from Cael Westerling, Senior DARPA supervisor in DC. He, along with six other major intelligence and White House heavyweights, were on the call.

Mason cleared his throat. "Ah sir, we have two primaries and three that were considered peripheral to the original target. The rest are acceptable collateral damage. In our run-up tabletop exercises for the program, the numbers were much higher. We're optimistic that our body count will be relatively low."

"So since this began," continued Westerling, "five individuals have died?"

"That's correct, sir.'

There was a long pause on the phone, "So how well is this being contained?" asked Jim Casswell, Chief of Staff at the DIA. "Have we had any media flashes? We're dark now, and I want this program to stay that way."

Mason had only met the man once at an Intel briefing at the Forrestal Building in DC last summer and had taken an immediate dislike to the man. He had the face and jerky mannerisms of an impatient weasel or ferret, someone whose natural tendencies were curt and condescending. He was a skinny long-distance runner who ran or rode his five-thousand-dollar Trek mountain bike the seven miles to work every day, a fitness snob considering anyone not equally fit a second-class slacker. The fact he had risen to such a high-level position at the DIA was evidence in Mason's mind that God just was not paying attention.

"It's being controlled without any problems," replied Mason, taking off his glasses and rubbing his eyes. He could already feel a headache starting to build. Caswell had a way of asking questions he already knew the answers to. As before, Mason could sense major insecurity in the man's personality, a flaw masked by being petty and officious.

George Hobbs, Chief Executive officer with the National Intelligence Agency and most senior of the men in both experience and age came on the line. "Mason, is the timeline still viable? What about those in your ranks you have had to cull, as it were, from this operation? Is there an exposure risk?"

"Sir, I assume you're are referring to Delany?"

"That's correct."

Mason quickly scanned the action brief he had received that afternoon. "Sir, he is currently under surveillance by two of our field units after being exposed to the enhanced array yesterday at 1600 hours. As far as our timeline for initiation, we are on schedule and should be launching at 1745 hours on the 19th, which is Thursday, two days from now."

"Are we still going with the Akashic Record and the Drake Equation as target data?" asked Hobbs.

"Yes, sir. As you know both of those subjects are obscure enough in themselves and present a very high profile trigger tag available to scan in the media. All systems are green and standing by for the launch. We are projecting actionable data showing up within 30 minutes of initiation."

John Tolliver, a Senior Operational officer with the NSA spoke up. "George, we're going to be using an enhanced spectrum scan, similar to the Bin Laden software. The collection will be within the Terra Bite range."

"That's correct," added Mason. "If those two trigger tags are mentioned anywhere in the media, we will pick it up."

Mason looked over the notes he had written up before the meeting. "Gentlemen, I am assuming you have all received your shielding lenses?"

"Yes," replied Hobbs. "And just to be clear, we are only going to be transmitting for six hours on the 19th, is that correct?"

"Yes, sir. If you are driving and are exposed to any traffic light in the designated areas, you will need to wear the lenses to prevent exposure. We will also be transmitting on the 23rd and the 28th from 1600 to midnight respectively."

"Mason," questioned Caswell, "what would be the result if one of us is exposed to the beam?"

Mason thought for a moment. "Well, sir, you, like every other person exposed, would be unable to stop thinking about the Akashic Record and the Drake Equation for several months. You would be another data point." *Jesus Christ,* he thought, *what did he think would happen? Twit.*

Mason could hear several of the men chuckling in the background. "All right, gentlemen," announced Hobbs, "if there are no other questions, I suggest we end this. I have a meeting with oversight on the Hill, and I'm already late. And, Jim, wear your glasses on the 19th, son."

Not a group much on conversation salutations, Mason could hear the men disconnecting from their locations. The call had gone pretty much as expected and nothing new had been dropped in his lap. Timelines were still solid, and all the players were standing by. It was a bonus that Delany was now nothing more than a passing footnote, soon to be forgotten as anyone who mattered to the program - so much for being the god-dammed golden boy.

Within his slow but steady rise in the organization, Mason knew that this was, by far, the biggest, most progressive gamble the community had made in gaining control of the country. He was honored to be a part of the effort yet profoundly fearful that if circumstances changed in the near future, if he became a threat to the group, he might find himself dealt with just like Delany. He knew the men at today's meeting would not hesitate to give the order. They were not his friends. They would not save him. Of this he was sure.

****

"Dave, wake up, my friend. C'mon Dave. Dave Portia, open your eyes."

Portia slowly opened his eyes and focused on a face he had never seen before. The man leaning close had kind eyes, the faint smell of stale coffee on his breath.

"Wha.. Where am I?"

The man smiled and stepped back, cocking his head slightly. "Glad to see you're awake, Dave. I'm Doctor Balis. You're in All Saints Hospital in Racine. Do you remember what happened?"

Portia shook his head. "No, I ,I, don't know what's going on. What happened?"

"Well, you had a pretty serious car accident," replied the man, picking up a clipboard near the foot of the bed. "Ah, let's see. Looks like you fractured your left shoulder, several ribs on your left side and you took a pretty heavy whack to the side of your head. It took twelve stitches to close it up. I've got you set up for an MRI later on today and a consultation with an orthopedist tomorrow about your shoulder."

Portia slowly tried to raise his right arm but was stunned to see that it was handcuffed at the wrist to the metal rail of the gurney. "Wha, What is this?"

The man set the clipboard on the small table by the bed. "Yeah, that. The police arrested you on suspicion of drunk driving. The officer is in the hall. I'll let him talk to you about that. I'll check in on you in a bit."

Just as he left, a young uniformed officer passed him in the doorway and stepped into the room. "Mister Portia, I see you're awake," he announced walking up close to the bed. "I'm going to read you your rights. Do you understand?"

Portia tried to sit up, but the pain in his shoulder flashed through his back, taking his breath away. "Jesus," he moaned settling back. "Am, am I under arrest? For what?"

The young officer pulled a small card from his uniform shirt pocket. "Sir, I need you to listen to what I am about to say. You have the righ…."

"God-damnit?" shouted Portia. "What the hell is going on? Why am I here? What happened?"

"Mister Portia," continued the officer calmly, "you have the right to remain silent. Anything you say can and will be used against you in a court of law. You have the right to an attorney. If you cannot afford an attorney, one will be appointed to you. Do you understand your rights?"

"Yes, I understand my rights. Now, will you please tell me why I am here and handcuffed to this god-damned bed?" He jerked his wrist against the cuff, sending another heavy jolt of jagged pain down his back. "Son of a bitch," he hissed.

The officer thought for a moment. "So, you really don't know what happened?"

Portia shook his head. "No, I do not."

"Professor, about two hours ago, you drove your car backward out of a parking lot at about 40 miles an hour."

"So, how is that a crime?"

The officer opened a small notebook. "Professor, you hit three other cars, causing major damage. When other officers arrived at the scene, you fought with them, got back in your car, and tried to flee. You then drove back across the parking lot and were hit by a Fed Ex truck going west on Eleventh Street. That's how you received those injuries." He closed the notebook. "You're lucky to be alive, sir. Hit and run, reckless driving, resisting arrest, and then causing another accident with an injury to the other driver."

" I, I don't remember any of that, I... "

"Sir, were you drinking?" interrupted the officer. "Your blood is being tested now; it's best to be truthful."

"No, absolutely not. That's ridiculous."

"Drugs, prescription or otherwise, the blood test will show if you had anything in your system."

"No, I do not take drugs, for God's sake."

"Then, sir, how would you account for your out-of-control behavior?"

"Listen to me, Officer. I am a responsible adult. I do not drink and drive, and I am not a drug user. I don't remember any of this."

The officer thought for a moment. "Okay, just for argument's sake, what is the last thing you remember?"

He took a deep breath and closed his eyes, trying to pull up the memory. "I remember leaving my office and getting in my car. There was this guy at my window and then I, I saw the angel." He said the words before he could stop them. "I, I mean, I think I saw…"

"You saw an angel? That's your story?"

"Officer, I know how that sounds but I.."

"No, professor, I don't think you do. If you were having hallucinations, there had to be a reason. Normal people do not see angels."

At that instant, the starkly vivid image of the messenger flashed through Portia's mind, nearly taking his breath away. It was as clear and compelling as it was when it first appeared.

As a tear rolled past his cheek, he looked up at the incredulous face of the officer, knowing, at that moment, that no matter what he said he saw, he would not be believed. He closed his eyes and took a deep breath. "I'm sorry, but it's the truth, Officer. I don't remember anything after seeing the angel."

The officer quietly nodded and then put the small notebook back in his pocket with a sigh. "Well Professor, here's the deal. Considering the charges you're facing and the concern shown by the University officials, let's hope that angel remembers seeing you. You're going to need all the help you can get."

Chapter Twelve - Best Plans

It was twelve hours before the initiation of Ground Star and, feeling restless, Mason was driving his new Ford 350 into the country, letting the scent of the wild sage of the badlands drift through the window. The scent was the comforting smell he needed, but it reminded him of his father.

His father's approval had meant the world to him, and he winced at the knowledge that his dad, a real hard-core, old-school moral heavyweight, wouldn't stand behind the deceptive line of the project. He was the kind of man who would just as soon cut out his own tongue than to lie.

Even at the end of a vicious three-year battle with cancer, the senior Mason, half the man in size at one hundred pounds, never lost the big picture of living in God's will, refusing the morphine drip that could have eased him so that he could be present with his family as he struggled in his final hours. His father, a man of herculean willpower, had carried the air of German stoicism and unmatched control, providing the measure of ethical behavior by which Mason had lived for many years.

It was four-thirty in the afternoon, and it was a good time to be alive in this part of the country. The sun provided a slightly muted light casting long shadows, a clear indicator of the changing season. The unease he felt thinking of his old man marred the afternoon.

He had called home before leaving the office, hoping to catch his wife. She would be running errands, going to pottery class, or shopping with friends. He smiled as he thought of all the slightly lopsided pots, oddly-colored plates, and mismatched cups that she had brought home with a childlike giddiness to display throughout the house.

He looked over at the boxed pair of prescription shielding glasses he had ordered for his wife. They had been married for over twenty years, and protecting his wife from what was about to happen was weighing heavy on his conscience.

On behalf of those who dictated the project, his orders to the team were to do nothing to shield family and friends. Anyone without the project security clearance could potentially become part of the unavoidable collateral damage in this operation, casualties for the collective good. Even with all his power and back-channel influence within the organization, his mandate had been the same. How would he, without breaking security protocol, convince her to wear the glasses on the release date to protect her from the transmitted collective memory?

In his twenty-three years of federal service, he couldn't think of any prior incident or operation that had held the potential of directly affecting anyone in his family. He had ordered drone strikes, sanctioned wet operations on friendly soil, and rendered Iraqi prisoners to third-party detention centers, all without a second thought. This was different. As a good soldier, this time when he pulled the trigger, everyone he knew would be affected. In addition, if anything went sideways with the operation, he was the one who would be buried. There would be no walking back from this one; no heartfelt apology in the event of a project failure would be accepted at this level.

He felt certain that those above him, a surprisingly small handful of powerful people, would be giving glasses to their own families. After all, rank in the thin air of the fifth floor and in the halls of elected congressional officials did have its undeniable privileges

It was five-thirty when he pulled to a stop at the four-way, ten blocks from the house. If his wife had gotten home, she would have called him back by now. Evidently it was pot-throwing night, and she wouldn't be home until after seven. He turned toward town, considering the options of take-out and weighing picking up some extra beer. The thought of how the organization was about to change the perceptions and collective memory of his family, friends, and the community had drifted from his thoughts on the soft South Dakota breeze.

Chapter Thirteen - Clarity

It was seven-thirty in the morning in Stonington when Scott stepped down from the eighteen-wheeler. He had been just outside Indianapolis a day earlier when he hitched the ride in the truck delivering machine parts to the Hancock County Yard near Stonington. The driver, a young guy named Mitch from Davenport, Iowa, had been kind enough to drop him downtown before heading out to finish the job.

Upon arrival, Scott felt more confused than let down. Absent was the anticipated triumphant walk in ethereal sunshine foretold by the vision, a vision that had faded dramatically in the last twelve hours. He adjusted the shoulder straps of the backpack and pulled his collar tight against the morning chill carried on a slow but persistent breeze heavy with the smell of saltwater.

He crossed the street as an early morning garbage truck clamored toward him, its long mechanical arm picking up the big brown cans and dumping the contents into the back with practiced precision. Scott motioned to the driver as he pulled up across the street. "Morning, I am looking for breakfast. Is anything open this early?" he shouted over the rumble of the truck's engine.

The driver put the truck in park and pointed out the window behind him. "Yeah. Head down School Street. You will find The Edge Water Café is open, just a couple of blocks down."

"Thanks."

The driver nodded, put the truck in gear and continued up the block.

As Scott walked, he realized that the hard drive he felt from the vision over the last several days had changed. The strong visceral pull had been replaced by a manageable, oddly crystalized memory, much like the sense of something following a traumatic event.

He saw the Edge Water Café sign and then stopped, suddenly realizing that he no longer felt the emotional need to keep moving. In fact, he now felt foolish for believing the vision in the first place. *What the hell am I doing here*, he thought looking back down the road. *Why did this happen? What is the purpose?*

Had he self-generated the vision? Had this all been a form of mental breakdown induced by booze and grief? *Shit,* he thought, spitting in the street. *What now?*

He was down to forty-three dollars and sixteen cents, did not know a soul in town, and had no place to stay. In a small town, he would stick out like a sore thumb, moving around without purpose. He wondered what the New England jails were like.

He suddenly longed to be back in his dingy room at the Mission. At least there he had a roof over his head and a bed to sleep in. He shook his head looking back up the street, knowing Fat Mike had given his room to someone else. All he had now was a backpack full of dirty clothes and just enough money to stay fed for a few days. For the first time since the vision, he felt the need for a drink.

The craving was back and growing, old dark sensations were beginning to bubble up as he headed towards the café. *If this is going to be the place where it all starts again, then this will be where it all ends*, he thought stepping into the warm, brightly lit café.

"Good morning. Sit anywhere," announced the older waitress looking up from the cash register on the other side of the room. "I'll be with you in a minute."

Scott nodded, dropping his backpack by the full coat rack and slid into a booth by the window. Surprisingly, there were quite a few people already seated and having breakfast. The breakfast crowd reflected the diversity of a typical working class town, the attire running the gamut from business suits and shined shoes to well-worn Carhart jackets and work boots.

The waitress approached with a menu tucked under her arm and a coffee pot in each hand.

"Regular or de-caff, hon?"

Scott turned the cup over that was sitting on the placemat. "Ah, regular would be fine."

The woman poured the coffee, laid the menu on the table and left as quickly as she had come. Her movements seemed effortless as she moved through the crowd of tables, engaging each diner with a quick word as she topped off their coffee. He recognized that she had something he had always wanted – to be a part of place, part of the fabric that made a hometown.

Outside on the wet streets, the morning traffic had picked up, a steady stream of people heading to work and buses laden with children heading to school. He watched, lost in thought, caught by surprise when two men suddenly slid into the seat across from him. Each man, appearing to be in the mid to late forties, heavy set, and dressed in a dark suit and tie, exuded the unmistakable air of someone in law enforcement.

"Hi Scott, mind if we join you?" It may have been a question, but the tone and movement belied the lack of a request.

"Who are you guys?" replied Scott with a sigh. "How do you know my name?"

The man pulled out a small notebook and a small manila envelope the thickness of a deck of playing cards.

"Scott, my name is Abbott. This is Mister Bonetti. Sorry for dropping in on your breakfast like this but we need to talk."

"Sooo, you guys cops, insurance, salesman, what?"

The waitress walked up before the man could answer. "Have you decided on what you want?" she asked taking her pad from her apron.

Abbott touched the waitress lightly on the arm and smiled. "One check, my dear. This is on me."

Too tired to argue and intuitively knowing that leaving without talking to the men was not an option, he handed the menu to the waitress. "Steak and three eggs over easy, hash browns, wheat toast, a large orange juice and ah, one of those muffins in the case over there."

"Blueberry okay?"

"That will be fine, ma'am."

"How would you like your steak?"

Scott looked back at the men and smiled. "Well done. Looks like we'll be here for a while."

"And for you two?" asked the waitress still scribbling on the pad.

Abbott smiled. "You, know what? Steak and eggs sounds good. I'll have the same."

The man called Bonetti spoke up. "Just waffles for me and coffee."

"Syrup, jam?"

"Syrups fine, ma'am. Thank you."

'Thank you, gentlemen. I'll get this right up," she announced, stuffing the pad back into her apron pocket.

As the waitress walked away, Abbott leaned forward smiling. "Sounded like you were ordering your last meal."

"I don't know, did I?" He sat back studying the two, "Who the hell are you guys and what do you want? I'm really not in the mood for any cloaked businessman bullshit."

Abbott sat back with a sigh. "Been a long trip, huh Scott? How are you feeling?"

"Who are you guys?"

Abbott looked around the room before continuing. "Headaches, numbness in the hands or feet anyth…?"

"Am I under some kind of arrest?" interrupted Scott. "Because if not, I'm calling the cops."

Abbott slid the small packet across the table. "We know what you've been through, Scott. We have been monitoring your travel here, all the way from Missouri. You've made it."

"What do you think you know about me, Abbott, if that's even your real name? Enlighten me."

Abbott opened the small notebook. "Your name is Scott Shore. You're forty-four-years-old and your last known residence was the Sisters of Mercy Mission in North Saint Louis. Six days ago you were exposed to a certain device that gave you a vision, a dream, as it were, to come to Stonington, Maine. You arrived here this morning. How am I doing so far, Scott?"

Scott paused, trying to decide if he could actually push his steak knife through Abbott's throat faster than Bonetti could stop him. "Are you the one that put that, that thing in my head?"

Abbott closed the notebook. "The project is a classified program, a study if you will. Only a small cross-section of Americans have been exposed to it. Others have…"

"Cross section of Americans?" interrupted Scott. "You mean you've done this to other homeless drunks?" he slammed his hand on the table. "Who the hell are you guys? Goddamnit, I want some answers."

Several diners turned toward the commotion but quickly returned to their meals.

Abbott pulled a leather credential wallet from his suit coat pocket and laid it on the table. "Open it and keep your voice down. I won't tell you again."

Scott took the wallet and looked at the ID and badge. "Okay. What does the DIA have to do with all of this?" he asked, handing it back. "I thought you guys were only chasing rag-heads in the Middle East."

The waitress brought the plates of food just as Bonetti was about to say something.

"Here you are, gentlemen. Can I get you anything else? More coffee?"

"Yes, ma'am, coffee," replied Abbott. "Thank you."

She refilled the cups and as she walked away Bonetti spoke. "There is a lot about this operation that we cannot discuss but we can tell you that your involvement is over. There's ten-thousand dollars cash in that envelope. It's yours."

"Why are you just giving me ten thousand dollars? Hell, I was told I was chosen. *Special* sounds worth a lot more than ten grand to me."

"Consider it a pain and suffering donation," replied Abbott cutting his steak. "You look like you could use it. What do you have left, twenty-five bucks and change in that zip lock of yours?"

"Fuck you, Abbott. I did not agree to any of this. You put something in my head that made me come here. That's a goddamned assault. It's criminal."

Abbott took in a large forkful of egg and steak and smiled. "Listen, asshole", he said with a full mouth. "Here's what the program did for you. It gave you a very nice dream with lots of pretty colors. Got your ass out of North Saint Louis. It looks like it even helped with your drinking. Now the kicker, it put ten grand in your pocket. Hell, Scott, you ought to be thanking us."

Scott thought for a moment still not sure how to process what he was hearing. "Thanking you for giving me hallucinations? You guys got a lotta balls saying that shit. So what now? What am I supposed to do?" he asked leaning close, still thinking about the steak knife.

"What do you mean?" replied Abbott.

"I mean, I'm in Maine for, Christ's sake. I don't know anybody here. Where am I supposed to go?"

"Go anywhere you want," replied Bonetti flatly. "You've got ten-grand. Buy a bus ticket."

Scott took the envelope off the table and put it in his coat pocket, still not sure he was going to keep it. "So now, that's it? We just go our separate ways? Is that it? In two years I get brain cancer from whatever you assholes exposed me to. What then?"

Abbott sat back and put his fork down with a sigh. "Here's the deal, Scott. You were part of an experiment, a very important experiment. Yeah it's kind of shitty that you did not know what you were a part of, but a lot of classified ops are not known to the general public. Deal with it. You got paid for what we think your time was worth. As far as the government's position goes, on their behalf, we thank you. Now it's time to move on. If that's not good enough for you, I'll take you out back, stuff your lame ass in the trunk of my car and drive it off the dock with you in it. Trust me, you will not be missed." He picked his fork back up and smiled. "Okay there, chief?"

"You really think you could do that? You don't know a thing about me, about what I have done in my life."

Abbott nodded. "Ah, I don't care, Scott. This is not a debate, just a message being delivered. As far as taking you out, I would not even break a sweat, ole buddy."

Scott sat back in his seat amazed at the man's palatable hostility and authoritative arrogance. "What if I went to the press, told them about this? Aren't you guys worried about that?"

"What are you going to tell em?" replied Abbott through a mouthful of food. "You had a vision to go to Maine, to meet some messiah, a vision the government somehow beamed into your head? Yeah, good luck with that. Let us know how that turns out. No, it's over. Take the money and move on."

"How many others were exposed to this vision? What was the point? What if I don't take the money?"

Abbott chuckled. "The *point* is way above your pay grade, Scott. As far as others go, hell, you said it yourself - you're special. You're the only one left. Concerning the money, people further up my food chain think you ought to be paid for services rendered. Plus, if anybody actually did believe your story, our side can say you were paid for participating in the experiment. Take the money, don't take the money. I couldn't really give a shit less."

Bonetti nodded in agreement while sipping his coffee. "Move on, Scott. This is the last courtesy call you're going to get. We are holding all the cards here. You will do nothing and say nothing because no one will believe you." He looked over at Abbott who was taking in the last bite of food. "I think we are done here."

Abbott nodded. "Yep, you're right, partner." He looked up at Scott as he pulled a hundred dollar bill from his wallet and tossed it on the table. "Consider yourself briefed, ole buddy. In the future you'll probably get a call from some head shrinker types, you know, folks who want to know how you're getting on, just to make sure you haven't jumped off a roof or something."

He slid out of the booth, as Bonetti stepped out. "Take care of yourself, Scott, " he announced pulling on his overcoat. "Bus station is three blocks down on the right. Have a nice life."

Just before leaving Abbott leaned in, "Count yourself lucky pal. You're still alive. Others weren't so fortunate." He winked and walked away as quickly as he had arrived.

It was a solid half hour before Scott slipped on his rucksack and stepped out into the early morning sunshine. It had taken him that long to process what he had been told.

As he slowly headed up the street, he felt an odd sense of closure. A weight had been lifted. At least he knew he wasn't having some kind of break down. He had been assaulted, and it had been out of his control. The only issue now was what to do about it. Getting on a bus and disappearing was a non-starter. The DIA, Bonettii, Abbott and whoever else was involved with this crap could go fuck themselves.

No, for now a shower, a bed and about twelve hours of sleep were needed. After that, he'd figure out his next move. *So much for clarity*, he thought spotting the Super 8 Motel sign several blocks ahead. *So much indeed.*

***

Eight hours later, at twenty-two thousand three-hundred and thirty-two miles above the earth, the wide band, Global Sat-Com Five satellite in its geosynchronous orbit began transmitting a binary coded message programmed weeks earlier to every open source receiver at selected sites throughout the continental United States. To the DARPA engineers and techs watching from the command center in South Dakota, it was a flawless transmission uplink. It could not have gone smoother.

Project **Ground Star** had begun.

Chapter Fourteen - Results

Preston Dell was late for work again. He had been late every day this week, completely out of character for him. In fact, he could normally be counted on to be 15 minutes early for his shift.. If Preston was anything, he was predictable - same parking space for nine years, same worn-out Levi jacket, same grey plastic lunch box with the red and black *Sig Saur firearms* sticker on top.

He hadn't been able to sleep since his wife had left to visit her sister in Dayton. Lacking her presence, the house was just too quiet. The woman was always getting up to pee or getting something to snack on or drink. He just couldn't rest without the sounds normally noticed half asleep, sounds that reminded him of her. Thankfully, she would be driving back Sunday and things at the house would get back to normal.

At sixty, he was one of the oldest machinists working the floor. He had declined several suggested promotions and the opportunity to move upstairs into one of the management cubicles over the years, stating he'd rather be shot in the face than move into one of those grey boxes.
He sat impatiently waiting for the light to turn, thinking of the day ahead when a thought flashed through his mind like a lightning bolt. Two words came to mind that he had never put together before - *Akashic Record.* Not only had he never seen it or said it, he had no idea what it was or even if it was actually a thing. Most troubling, the two words suddenly occupied every bit of his attention, even making it difficult to focus on driving.

With some effort, he pulled into his normal parking space and then sat behind the wheel trying to remember where he was and what he was doing. Shaking his head, he put his truck in park and turned off the engine, fighting the urge to cry, something he hadn't done since he put down his twelve-year-old black lab Biscuits two years ago. "Jesus Christ," he whispered, "what the hell is going on?"

Finally gaining a level of control, he stepped out of his truck and, to his stunned surprise, noticed that half of his fifteen coworkers were still sitting in their vehicles.

****

Mason had been up most of the night. After telling his wife that she needed to wear the protective glasses, he found himself explaining to her why. Her reaction had been as he would have expected. She firmly condemned the whole thing, saying the government had no right playing god with the thoughts and thinking of the American public. She had been resolute in her disappointment in him, a man of integrity, for any part he had in the ghastly intelligence services overreach. The arguing had gone on well past midnight, coming to an abrupt end when she stomped upstairs and slammed the bedroom door. The discussion had left him ill-at-ease with the inability to fall asleep until three o'clock in the morning.

He swiped his key card through the card reader at the first security gate on his way to the office. He was surprised how good he felt after that first cup of coffee despite only having four hours sleep. Ground Star had been up and running for at least eight hours and he was anxious to get to his office and start reading the data. The people up the food chain would want the information as soon as possible.

"Hey, Mason, turn around. I've been waiting for you."

He stopped just short of the second security door and turned to the familiar voice.

Mason dropped his briefcase and slowly raised his hands, his eyes wide and fixed on the pistol in Delany's hand.

"You know I have to do something about what's going on. I can't let this continue."

"Jesus, Rob, put the goddamned gun down. Let's talk about this."

"It stops here," Delany said, holding the gun firmly, his back stiff with resolve.

He pointed to the CCTV box on the wall behind him. "You can't get away with this. The security cameras are recording everything, Rob. This isn't going to stop anything. C'mon, let's talk."

Delany took a step closer. "Talk? You took away everything I worked for. You tried to destroy me with the amplified array. What the hell is there left to talk about, Mason? Do you think I came here to negotiate, asshole? We're way past that now."

Mason looked over his shoulder as several more cars pulled into the employee parking lot behind him. He knew that few if any of the people working at the site carried weapons in their cars. He looked back at Mason, confident that a good Samaritan wouldn't come to stop anything.

Techs were exiting their cars, and Mason could see the fearful, confused looks as they recognized the situation. "Listen, Rob, just put the gun down and let's…" Bam! A 40-caliber slug suddenly ripped through his neck, dropping him to the pavement with a groan, the shot echoing off the front of the concrete building. A heartbeat later, Delany drew a deep shuddering breath, stepped up and stuck the barrel of the Glock through the chain link fence, firing six more times into Mason's lifeless body lying three feet away.

The security camera in the TOC two floors down had been a witness to the entire event. The five man QRF team, in a jingle of keys and weapons, were now pounding up the stairway on their way to the scene but would be far too late to affect the outcome.

Just before he stepped off that final ledge, Delany saw in his mind's eye, the billowing white robes of the Angel descending from an aura of golden sunshine. He smiled at the beautiful lie, no longer hearing the words of redemption. At the speed of a bullet, he had moved past the very real boundaries of no return. He put the barrel in his mouth and blew a three-inch hole out the top of his head.

***

The DIA headquarters, a sprawling black glass and white concrete structure was located on the premises of Joint Base Anacostia –Bolling in DC, a twenty-minute drive from Arlington, Virginia. Caswell's phone began to ring in his office on the sixth floor before the blood and brain matter had even been washed off the pavement in South Dakota.

"Caswell."

"We have a problem in South Dakota." Caswell immediately recognized the voice of George Hobbs, Director of National Intelligence.

"What kind of problem?" Caswell pulled up his office chair and sat down, still in his biking shorts from the ride in.

"You know the guy Mason kicked off Ground Star, Robert Delany? He just shot and killed Mason in the DARPA parking lot and then shot himself in the head."

"Holy shit! When did this happen?"

"About an hour ago. Bad business all around," replied Hobbs. He had been exposed to the amplified array. Everyone hit by that thing goes off the deep end. I am assuming the effects on Delany were no different."

Caswell thought for a moment. "Does this have any blowback for us?"

"I don't see how," replied Hobbs. "The press will be contained as always. The story is - just another workplace violence incident that just happened to take place at a government facility. I really don't see much of a problem. Make sure the bodies of both are transferred to our facility. The ME here will be performing the autopsies. The families will be notified of the results after the brain scans are complete."

Caswell checked his watch. "All right. It's noon there. I'm going to go ahead and contact Mason's 2IC and have all of his files and secondary media secured. I think his name is Rosten, Rositer, something like that?"

"Rolstein," corrected Hobbs. "He's another one of those Berkley boys. Seems solid. Met him at the DARPA conference last year in Savannah."

"Is he someone we can move up? We're going to need eyes-on out there."

Hobbs thought for a moment. "I'll get back to you on that. Let's see how well this first phase of Ground Star goes. If the matrix brings in the kind of numbers we think it will, we can discuss Rolstien's position again."

"Just to be thorough," replied Caswell turning on his laptop, "I'll contact the Sioux Falls FBI office immediately and have them take control of the local investigation. The national security asset involvement at a classified facility gives us cover in case the family starts to bitch."

"When you contact them, make sure they get to Delany's home ASAP and clean it out. We don't need whatever problems he had with Mason showing up on an unsecured computer somewhere. I don't want some cow-country sheriff or local police chief trying to make a name for himself at our expense. Shut it down - all of it."

"All right. I'll start making phone calls," replied Caswell. "'Ground Star has been online now for a solid eight hours. We should start seeing data. The media people are on it as we speak. I'll have a prelim report by this afternoon."

"That's fine. Keep me posted. I'm heading over to the Senate this afternoon but should be done with that hearing by three. Contact me with the numbers."

"Ah, tough break about Mason, huh?" replied Caswell.

"Yeah, well these things happen, but we need to keep our focus. Mason was a good soldier but replaceable. Let's keep our eye on the ball. Get me those numbers by this afternoon. Higher is going to want to see them."

"Okay. I'm on it."

***

Between ninth and twelfth street, across from the Museum of American African Art in DC is the James Forrestal building, a large, six-floor grey stone structure housing the headquarters for the Department of Energy and the Maryland Commerce Department.

Just off the lobby entrance, past the security check-in station and metal detectors, was a nondescript unmarked metal door, accessing the first level basement and a short brightly lit hallway that lay 40 feet below 9th street. This hall led to a second door which opened to a large air-conditioned room filled with seven, refrigerator-sized mainframe servers.

The IT tech, a young grad student from Georgetown, hired for one specific task, sat with his feet on the only desk in the room watching the latest tag feed from all five of the social media outlets. He had been in the room since six-thirty that morning watching the tag feed tic by. His only mandate - to log the number of hits registering *Akashic Record* or *Drake Equation*.

He typed in the codes for the matrix collation and after a moment received a detailed breakdown. Never in his twenty-eight years on the planet, had he seen such a rapid and large cross-demographic subject-tag hit. As he watched the numbers continuing to grow, he punched in the DIA headquarters' number. The phone was answered on the second ring.

"Caswell."

"Ah yes, sir. This is Linder over at Forrestal. I have a fairly sizable amount of data available. You said you needed it quickly."

"That's correct. Can you send me the data?" replied Caswell.

"Yes, sir. It's on the way right now." Linder touched the *send* prompt.

"Thank you. Linder. The file just came up on my screen."

"Sir, you need to know that there are 18 pages to that file, interest in two subjects I have never even heard of. It's crazy."

There was a pause on the phone, leading Linder to think that Caswell had disconnected.

"Sir, sir are you there?"

"'If you don't mind me asking, Linder, how did you get to work this morning?"

"Ah, I took the metro - green line. I don't have a car." He answered the strange question.

"Okay. Go ahead and keep monitoring the data."

"Sir, can I ask you a question?"

"Sure."

"Sir, according to this data, a little over twelve million people and counting are looking into the Akashic Record and the Drake Equation. Sir, I have never heard of either. I was wondering if you have?"

There was a pause on the phone, an uncomfortable silence.

"Hey, Linder,"

"Yes, sir."

"Are you looking to get into the intelligence field once you're out of school?"

"Yes, I was planning on it. That's why I took this job. I'm hoping that it might look good on the resume."

"You're on the right track. Just keep sending me updates."

"Yes, sir. Will do and thank you for the opportuni..." The call was disconnected before he could finish.

Shit, he thought, tossing his phone on the desk, *nothing like making a first impression.* He looked back at the screen as the numbers continued to grow. "Amazing," he whispered.

Chapter Fifteen: Landing

The ocean held a certain kind of soul-based magic, a heartfelt draw for Scott that he could not explain. He had never lived near it though he would have liked to. His salary had always been way too thin to buy a home even within sight of a beach so his exposure had come through short expensive vacations.

Now, with life at a physical and emotional crossroads, he stood on a dock letting the cold salty air blow into his face as the late afternoon sunset painted the sky a faded purple. Seagulls squawked and drifted in the stiff breeze overhead as several small fishing boats puttered away trailing blue-white exhaust into the harbor, past the long grey stone breakwater, a hundred yards away.

It had been two days since his encounter with the *Agents*. Rested, fed, and cleaner than he had been in weeks, he wiggled his toes in the new socks and boots and smiled at the possibilities. Part of the cash had paid for a two-week stay at the motel, a set of new clothes from the small store downtown, and comfort food and snacks that now stocked the mini-fridge in his room. A roof overhead, clothes on the back, and food for the belly, he had all the things that most people take for granted.

He had no real idea why he was staying in the area but trying to get revenge or justice for what had happened to him seemed unachievable. As much as it angered him, the agent had been right - who would believe anything from an alcoholic 'nobody'?

The vision, now only a faded memory, held no power over him. Watching one of the boats ease up to the dock, a question surfaced in his mind. What was so bad about being here? Why shouldn't he stay? There was nothing for him back in Saint Louis.

One of the fishing boats slowly maneuvered towards the dock, its deck stacked high with lobster traps and coiled ropes. One of the crew stepped off the rail as it drew close and quickly tied a stern line to the dock cleat. A second crewman appeared out of the small wheelhouse and, without a word, tossed a second line to the man on the dock, a dance that had been performed a thousand times before. The engine slowly sputtered to a stop as the boat eased gently up against the three large faded white plastic bumpers hanging off the side.

The man in the wheelhouse stepped out and lit a cigarette before hopping down onto the dock.

Scott smiled and nodded as the man approached. "You look like you've parked that boat a time or two."

The man grinned. "Yeah, well, once or twice," he replied walking by with the other man.

"Say, you wouldn't know of any work around here would ya?" called Scott after the men.

The man with the cigarette stopped and turned. "You know anything about fishing?" he asked blowing a lung full of smoke to the sky.

Scott shoved his hands deep in his new coat pockets. "Well, not really. Never worked on a fishing boat before."

The man flicked the cigarette off into the water. "The only real work here is fishing, my friend."

Scott stepped forward. "I ah, I have no real place to go and I'm a fast learner."

The man thought for a moment. "Season is almost over. Winter is coming on. No real time left to school a greenhorn."

The other man spoke up. "Besides, most of the fleets are going to be dry-docking boats for repairs and such. Bad time to look for a job." The men turned to walk away.

"When you dry dock, what's involved?" asked Scott.

The man with the cigarette turned with a sigh. "Lots of blood, sweat, tears, and money for hull repair, engine overhauls, painting, scraping, and shit like that."

Scott walked over to the men. "I'm a machinist - tool and die. Well, at least I used to be. That boat has a diesel engine, right?"

"Yeah, it does."

"I know my way around a diesel engine pretty well," announced Scott before he could stop the words.

The man thought for a moment and then looked over at his crewmate and winked.

"Okay, what do you know about a Caterpillar C8?"

"Marine?"

"Yep, about four years old."

"Well, if I remember right, it's an in-line six, puts out a little over 650 horsepower, about 2300 RPM at full gain, has a radial driven belt turbocharger compatible with most retrofit engines that Cat puts out, and a real workhorse. Yeah, I know a little bit about it. Is it giving you trouble?"

The man laughed to the sky. "I'll be damned." He walked over and extended his hand. "Name is Bing Deshane and you are?"

"Scott," he said shaking hands with both men. "Just got into town. Thought I would try and find a job."

Deshane looked over at his friend and then back to Scott. "What the hell brings you to Stonington, Maine? This dock is the far east edge of the United States, for Christ's sake."

Scott smiled. "It's a long story. Lost my wife some time back. Been wandering ever since." He had no idea why he was so forthcoming with complete strangers. He just had a nagging feeling that it needed to be said, that he needed to explain all this to someone, anyone.

Deshane thought for a moment. "Tell 'ya what. I'm about to freeze my ass off and I need coffee. Let's head up to the Head Water Café. We can talk about engines somewhere warm. I'm buying."

Scott smiled. "Appreciate that, Captain."

A strange look flashed across Deshane's face, a mixture of sadness and confusion.

"Well, I ain't the Captain," he said zipping up his coat. "That's a story in itself. Just call me Bing." He pulled his collar up around his neck. "C'mon, let's get out of this goddamned wind."

As the men walked, Scott sensed that something important had happened, a strange, undefinable goal had been reached. Maybe the vision had been right all along. He felt that he was having a resurrection back to the living. Hell, for all he knew, Deshane *was* the team leader he was supposed to meet. Who was he to question a miracle?

He had never worked on a diesel engine before in his whole life.

***

It was stunning how fast a well-manicured life could fall apart.

Portia had been released on bail after spending three days in the hospital but his reputation had been destroyed. He had been suspended from work with pay since the incident and was still waiting for the court hearing concerning his resisting arrest charge, something he still did not remember. Now, the job he loved was about to be taken from him by men he had once considered friends and colleagues. The meeting had been scheduled for two o'clock, and he fully expected it to be over by two-fifteen.

"So Professor Portia, as you know the university administration requested a board of inquiry into your accident and subsequent arrest. This is not a criminal court, of course. It is a hearing of your peers to determine your eligibility to continue teaching here. Do you have any questions before we start?"

Portia sat back in his chair with a sigh, knowing full well that the Regents had already made a decision concerning his fate. This was just another check-box formality. "I'm sure that senior staff has already made up their minds about this incident. I would just like to dispense with all the pretense."

Kathern Riddel, one of the University's recent law school graduates, spoke up from the other side of the table. Portia had met her once at a faculty mixer a year earlier. He was surprised that she had not moved on to bigger and better things, considering her age and ability.

"Professor, it's our intention to give you the opportunity to provide some kind of explanation concerning your case. I can assure you that there is no pre-judgment one way or another on this side of the table."

Portia thought for a moment. "Well, that's going to be a problem," he replied shifting the sling that held his casted left arm. "As I said before, I do not remember anything after I left work that afternoon - nothing. I cannot tell you how frustrating that is. I don't know what happened. I only know that I was attacked somehow."

Cranston Bell, the University's lead personnel administer, opened a file on the table. "Ah, Professor Portia, are you familiar with a woman by the name of Jessica Minor?"

Portia felt his heart skip a beat and the room grow noticeably hotter. "Yes, I know Miss Minor. She was one of my grad students last fall."

Bell slid the folder over to Riddel, who spoke up without looking at the paper, her tone full of sharp edges. "Professor Portia, Miss Minor said you pressured her into a sexual affair. She said she felt that your relationship with her was coerced for a favorable endorsement of her work."

"That's outrageous! Are you accusing me of sexual harassment? Is this what this is all about?" Even as he asked the question, he could feel the walls of his career starting to collapse. He would not walk away from this, no matter what he said in his defense. It was over.

"Professor Portia," replied Bell leaning back in his chair with a sigh, "we just need to hear your side of the story. Miss Minor has provided us with a rather detailed statement regarding this relationship and, for balance, we need to hear your side of this."

Portia thought for a moment, shaking his head. "Would it make a difference?"

Bell took off his reading glasses. "Would what make a difference?"

Portia smiled. "Giving you my side of the story. Would it change the outcome? You see, it's true Miss Minor and I had a brief consensual fling. No matter what it was at the time, this accusation will be judged in the current social construct. In this environment of sexual harassment head-hunting, I will be guilty no matter what happened."

Riddel began writing notes on a legal pad. "So you're admitting to having a sexual relationship with one of your students. Is that correct, Professor Portia?" she asked, not looking up.

"You heard what I said. We had a consensual relationship. It ended within months of starting. Do I regret it? Of course. Was anyone coerced? Absolutely not. Look, I'm done here. My arm is killing me and I need to get some air."

Riddel looked up from her pad. "Ah, Professor, I think we have a few more questions. I think it would be in your best...."

"My best interest?" interrupted Portia sliding his chair back. "Here's what is in my best interest: You go ahead and recommend termination for cause and I will not only sue this University for wrongful termination, but each of you individually. My tox report came back and as you all well know, no alcohol or drugs were found in my system. I may not win this case but I will tie you and this University up in court for years. I have nothing to lose. I am a tenured Professor at this institution with an impeccable record and I will have my day in court.

"Professor Portia," interrupted Riddel, "please sit down so we..."

"I'm not finished," snapped Portia. "As far as Miss Minor is concerned, if she wants to lodge a specific complaint in an official capacity, I suggest she do so. I will also not hesitate to drag her into court and have her explain, in detail, our sexual relationship. As far as this meeting is concerned, I have nothing more to say." He tapped the table for emphasis. "You do what you have to do. I assure you, I will." He walked out of the large conference room without closing the large double doors behind him.

He was bluffing, of course. He had no intention of going to court over this. He knew that it only took an accusation of sexual impropriety in today's cancerous, politically-correct environment to end a career. He was just tired of defending himself in a battle he could not win. He had more important things to do than sit before a group of people who had no right judging him in the first place.

He was responding to a higher order now - much higher.

As he stepped outside, he spotted his wife sitting behind the wheel of her car at the bottom of the steps. As he approached the passenger side window, he could see that she was greatly upset. Married for over a decade, he could read her moods without her having to say a word.

"Hi, Sweetheart. Thanks for waiting. I could've.."

"Is it true?" she interrupted, gripping the wheel while looking straight ahead.

"Is what true?"

She looked at him with a mixture of anger and pain, her eyes red and puffy from crying. "The intern, the girl you had an affair with last summer, is it true?"

He paused for a moment, his first reaction to ask how she had found out but checked himself. Nothing could be gained prolonging the inevitable. "Yes, it's true, all true, sweetheart. I really don't have any excuses for my…"

She backed the car away before he could finish the sentence. He didn't blame her for leaving. If the situation were reversed, he would have reacted the same way. He was guilty of betrayal at the highest order, and nothing he could say would change that. As he walked across the parking lot toward his rental car, he felt as if a thousand pounds had been lifted off his shoulders. There was nothing holding him back now.

All of his dark secrets, those he had been carrying around were now known. In an odd sense, he had never felt more free. He was ashamed for hurting his wife; she deserved better treatment. If she wanted to divorce him for this betrayal, he would support her decision.

Not able to contain his smile, he popped two more Darvocet pain pills, turned on the ignition, and recalibrated the GPS Garmin he had brought from home. Something miraculous had happened. Everything else in his life paled to that experience.

If he drove straight through, he could be in Stonington, Maine, in three days. The only thing that mattered now was getting on the road and heading east. The job would still be there or not. The wife would still be there or not. He had no control over either. There had been a monumental shift in his priorities.

The Angel had told him that he was special, that he was watched over. With that kind of direct divine providence on his side, nothing could stop him. By the time he hit the interstate, he was practically giddy with excitement about the future. His mind had never been more clear. He had never felt more blessed.

Chapter Sixteen - The Gathering Storm

Caswell hated having the meeting here, but it was the largest SCIF in the Forestal Building. The lack of windows in the basement made the room feel like an airless tomb, the large florescent lights adding to the depressive mood. The meeting had been called for nine but most of the attendees had been there since eight-thirty, a clear indication of the subject's importance. Caswell took his normal place at the table capable of seating twenty. He sat just off to the right of the table head.

"All right, gentlemen," began Caswell opening his leather portfolio, "we need to get started."

The attendees settled into their seats without the normal decorum of greetings and handshakes.

"I'll start by saying that most, if not all, of the antidotal data on Ground Star is in. The numbers on some of the other hard-side data from partners in the media are still being crunched, information that should be in by the close of business today. As a reminder, this information does not have a clearance listed as anything but TS within this area venue. Now, a bit of housekeeping is in order. Hobbs?"

George Hobbs, Director of National Intelligence added from the other side of the table, "It is agreed that most, if not all, of our wireless communications and e-networks within the DC metro are compromised. All of Ground Star hard data and operating concepts and matrix are currently running through our primary, stand-alone facility at Fort Gordon. The stand-alone system at Gordon gives us complete control over the information, providing a much higher level of security."

Caswell continued, "There, the program is listed under YANKEE WHITE security classification protocol and cannot be accessed remotely. Are there any questions or concerns about that?"

Robert Cranston, CIA Deputy Director and long-time supporter of Ground Star, spoke up. "If we want to see some of the information on the program, what is the procedure?"

Caswell looked up from his notes while removing his reading glasses. "You will have to physically go to Fort Gordon, be read into the information access table, and then you will have access to the information."

Cranston seemed satisfied with the answer and did not ask a follow-up.

"All right, we are now well into the second week of Ground Star operations, and the results are promising. Since the stop-light microbursts were brought online last Thursday, we have had a media hit count of over five hundred and sixty-eight million on one of the selected topics. On the second topic, we have had a response of over twenty million twenty-eight thousand thus far. Social media hits range from short duration one-time inquires to multi-informational gathering sessions, some lasting hours. Amazing, actually." Caswell sat back in his chair letting the information sink in.

"So the technology we are using has been successful?" questioned Hobbs.

Caswell looked back at his notes. "Considering the subject matter, the across-the-board population demographics responding, and the duration of the tests, yes. I would classify this as a success."

Hobbs thought for a moment. "What is the data on the enhanced array exposure?"

Caswell flipped through several pages of notes before answering. "Sir, as you know, that is the *weaponized* version of the array. To this date, six people have been exposed to that device."

"And the results of that exposure?"

Caswell cleared his throat. "Three had complete mental breakdowns proving fatal. Two others had severe mental psychosis that resulted in major lifestyle changes. One individual committed murder-suicide. That involved Director Mason at the DARPA facility in South Dakota. It is truly a weapon."

Hobbs sat back in his chair. "So both arrays are successful in their designated areas of operation?"

"That's correct. We could implement the weaponized array in any conflict zone as soon as thirty days from today. The wide spectrum exposure is devastating."

"Then what is stopping us from doing it?" questioned Cranston. "Christ, we could wipe out at least five hard-core terrorist groups that have been giving us shit for decades and get it done by Christmas."

Caswell smiled. "Gentlemen, all it takes to put the weaponized array into the United States military arsenal is a phone call from this room."

Cranston sat back in his chair shaking his head. "Jesus, George, make the call. I'd say we hit them with everything we've got."

To Caswell, the CIA Director's hair-trigger response was predictable and soundly unwise.

"Director, I don't think to send the second array into the ranks would be prudent at this time. Far more information needs to be gathered on both the long-term and short-term effects of the array. The science side of the operation is still gathering information through conferences and meetings. We just do not have a large amount of conclusive data."

"You just said it works and, in your words, would be devastating. What else do we need to know?" questioned Cranston, amazed that he was the only one speaking up.

"Well," replied Caswell, "there are several things we don't know yet. One - how long the effects last: a week, a month, two months? Secondly, there is an element of the unpredictable result. All the individuals exposed to the amplified array had different reactions. When exposed, they became unpredictable, emotional, and mental grenades."

"We don't have enough data on the second array to confidently roll it into any defense budget," announced Hobbs. "I do not want the enhanced array hardware in the hands of people we do not directly control. The risk is too great for an uncontrolled incident."

Cranston was undeterred. "Well, for the greater good, I suggest we do a large scale domestic test."

Hobbs nodded in agreement, knowing that every man sitting at the table would not think twice about ordering the enhanced array experiment on the general population. "I don't think that's out of order. We were able to control collateral damage before. I would suggest a thousand individuals, picked at random, of course. That would give us the information we need before proceeding on a larger scale."

"I disagree," replied Caswell. "The enhanced array is effective in causing a level of acute psychosis but the response is erratic at best. The unmodified array has shown to be far more effective in subliminal impute and is far more controllable."

"So what are you suggesting?" questioned Hobbs.

Caswell thought for a moment and then looked back at his notes. "I suggest that we use the stop-light medium to transmit nationwide control of the narrative on all issues such as the President's popularity, promoting the rise of selected politicians, directing social trends, with everything going through the filter of the collective good."

Hobbs leaned back in his chair. "You're talking about a very large roll up. What kind of time frame is needed before that could happen?"

"Now, hold on," announced Cranston, "I still think we need to discuss the second array, as far as.."

"I have the support people in place," interrupted Caswell "and the tech folks ready to pull the trigger. We can be up and running in 24 hours."

"Bullshit!" replied Cranston, shaking his head. "You can stand this thing up in twenty-four hours?"

"That's correct. I had expected that we would get the framework up and running on Ground Star within a week of its inception."

"So when will we have a meaningful discussion about the implementation of the enhanced array?" asked Cranston pointedly.

"We are having a discussion, Bob. We are.."

"Gentlemen, I think I need to interject something here," interrupted Hobbs. "We are not getting anywhere arguing. I want to remind everyone about the original concept of Ground Star. It was designed to implement a passive and effective method of population control. That is the bedrock concept of Ground Star."

Cranston shook his head. "But we now have a golden…"

"Let me finish, Bob," continued Hobbs. "The enhanced array was a secondary experiment pushed for and headed by Director Mason's DARPA group. He was the spearhead on that side of the project." Hobbs tapped the table for emphasis. "All of the effort, all of the money, and the lion's share of the technology expenditures have gone into the primary Ground Star mission."

Caswell closed his notebook and sat back, satisfied that his point of view was about to be confirmed. He hadn't gotten into this powerful position by kicking big stones on the career path, obviously, something Cranston had not figured out. In big-league political hardball, the rules of engagement changed by the hour.

As we have seen by the data from the program's first run," continued Hobbs, "Ground Star is now viable. I am approving implementation on a national scale and want our efforts focused in this direction."

"So, where does that leave the enhanced array?" asked Cranston, still not convinced the right decision had been made.

Hobbs continued, "The CIA will take over the program involving the enhanced array and will limit the number of subjects exposed for further study."

"What are those numbers?"

Hobbs thought for a moment. "A thousand individuals at the most. That number should give you the data needed with regard to both short and long term effects. Bob, I expect the program to stay within that parameter. Even with that, I think you're going to have your hands full. With that said, I need a comprehensive path forward from you as soon as possible, the implementation plan and cost analysis breakdown. I need them within the week."

Cranston seemed satisfied as he wrote in his notebook "What about the DARPA section? Will we have access to the full database of information. I want my folks to know the real guts of the technology."

Hobbs nodded. "I'll make the phone call as soon as we finish here." He looked around the room to the other attendees. "Does anyone else have a point they want to bring up?"

Cranston looked over at William Talbot, the acting FBI director. "Bill, I will get with you after we're done here to start working out the details of a mutual aid agreement."

Donovan Jewell, Senior Director of the Security Council spoke up from the far end of the table. "George, to ensure that we are all getting the same information and have equal opportunity to provide input to the Ground Star program, I think we need to have designated staff from each of our organizations permanently attached to the project. I have a few topic applications that I think we need consider. Favorable UN relations is an example."

Hobbs turned to Caswell. "Do you see any problems with the increased staff?"

Caswell shook his head. "No, sir. I was going to suggest the same thing. The office space will more than accommodate the additional personnel. That is assuming that the NSA complex will be used for running the program and that each organization won't be adding more than 3 additional individuals.

Caswell thumbed through several pages of notes before continuing. "As far as the subject matter goes, I suggest we start with favorable government attitudes in general. The government currently has a very low public opinion rating. I think we should start addressing this as it will lay the platform for the following topics. We will begin collecting specific transmission data points from each organization and run them in succession.

Hobbs nodded. "I agree. Gentlemen, I will need the list of the people you are going to send on my desk by close of business tomorrow. Start sending specific topics you would like to address by the end of next week." Hobbs closed his notebook.

"Gentlemen, I want to thank you all for your continued cooperation with this project. We are on the verge of finally having control of the national narrative on a wide range of matters. That in itself is a truly monumental feat. There will be challenges ahead, but through dedication and cooperation we will succeed. Thank you again. Now, unless anyone else has anything to add?" He looked at the men sitting quietly around the table.

Not one showed even a hint of trepidation about the course of action they were about to take. The moral firewalls concerning Ground Star had fallen away long ago. The balance of real power was about to be restored, and for the sixteen government representatives in the room, it could not happen fast enough.

As the room began to clear, Caswell caught Hobbs' eye, signaling that he had something else to say when the others were gone. Hobbs closed the door after the last man and took a seat at the now empty table.

"Is everything in order?" he asked as Caswell took a seat.

"Yes, sir. The transmit time-frames sent to the organization heads will be off by one day. Since then, we have intensified the array so that the protective glasses will not prevent exposure to the new messages. Everyone will receive the same information."

Hobbs paused and looked Caswell directly into the eyes. "I think Cranston is going to be a problem. He is way too eager to get his hands on the enhanced array. I foresee a control issue. In that vein, I propose that he should have some kind of *accidental* exposure, something that results in early retirement. The sooner the better."

Caswell nodded. "Yes, sir. Ah, you are aware that the others are going to realize that their thoughts are being manipulated as well. They're going to know that they have been exposed to the array. What is our answer when they start asking questions?"

Hobbs thought for a moment. "On an operation such as this, the fewer people that know about the inner workings the better. Trust me, there is way too much hubris within this group. Few are likely to admit having been affected by anything. As far as answering questions? I would suggest prudence. You have been brought into something very big and shiny, yet very dangerous. I'll leave it to you to decide what to say." Hobbs checked his watch.

"Christ, I'm late for a meeting on Capitol Hill. Anyway, green light the operation and start thinking of who would be a good fit for Cranston's position. We're going to need a real team player in the coming months. No tree huggers, no climate change dingbats, and no minorities, clear? Find a Bones man. We can always count on one of our own. Once you get a name, I'll put him through the committee on a fast track."

"Yes, sir. I'm on it. Sir, do we expect any interference from Congressional oversight or from the White House on this?"

Hobbs smiled faintly, "Not a bit. Administration in the White House has a maximum of eight years of moderate influence, an influence that we allow. Our plans and control extend a lot further than eight years. Concerning Congress, we paid for them a long time ago," He slowly pushed back his chair and stood up, straightening his tie. "Let's get this done, Jim. The sharpest knife cuts the cleanest."

"Yes, sir."

Caswell knew full well that if the Director could betray friends and people he had worked with for years this easily, that he faced a risk as well. Contrary to Hobbs' reassurance that he has his best interest at heart, that he is now a member of the inner circle - he knew it to be bullshit. Politics at this level was a blood sport. Anyone playing by the rules and the "Mister Smith goes to Washington" mindset of fairness, was quickly ground into a fine powder and blown back across the Potomac. Only predators survived in a town like Washington.

Casewell made his way towards the parking lot, recognizing that he was in a race against time. He knew his value to Hobbs would last only as long as it took to get the Ground Star operation up and running. The second the program was working on its own, he knew Hobbs would make a move to purge the original team. He would be among the *retired* and wounded. At this altitude of power, the air was too thin to share..

Before he slid into the backseat of his waiting car, he had already developed his planned move against Hobbs. It was a shame that no matter what action he took, it would be far too late.

Chapter Seventeen - From Flash to Bang

Donovan Jewell, the Security Council Director had just crossed the George Washington Bridge in his chauffeured black Lincoln when his cell phone buzzed in his pocket. He answered the expected call on the second ring.

"Hello."

"Donovan, our suspicions have been confirmed."

Jewell thought for a moment as the DC landscape rolled by outside. "All right, how extensive is the damage?"

The man on the other end of the line was Marcus Harper, National Reconnaissance Director and one of the sixteen in the meeting at the SCIF just an hour ago. He was also the one tasked with bugging the room prior to the meeting, a herculean feat accomplished with micro-monitoring devices he had personally carried into the room.

"I have the playback. It's not good. He and Caswell are taking us all out. It's irrefutable."

Jewell sighed heavily, feeling the full weight of his long-term friend's betrayal. Hobbs had been in his graduating class at Yale. Their respective careers had followed parallel paths to the top of the mountain in the intelligence service. He knew Hobbs' wife Clara and both of his grown daughters. He was a friend, making this all more painful.

Whether he would admit it openly or not, he had been suspicious of his friend for months now, recognizing the depressing fact that the more power Hobbs obtained, the more he wanted. The old saying that "power corrupts and absolute power corrupts absolutely" had proven bedrock true.

"Do you want me to initiate the measures?"

Jewell paused only briefly. "I hate doing this. The man is a real patriot."

"Was," replied Harper flatly. "No one man should have that much power. This is on him, Donovan. Don't beat yourself up over what we have to do."

"George and his family have been friends of mine for over thirty years. I just hate to see it end this way," replied Jewell.

"I understand but he has left us no other option. You and I both know this has been getting worse by the month. We simply do not have a choice."

Jewell shifted uneasily in his seat. He hated the decision he was about to make. "All right," he said with a sigh. "You have a green light. Make sure there isn't collateral damage. This needs to be clean."

"Not a problem. The team is standing by. This will be over in an hour."

"Has the rest of the organization been notified?" questioned Jewell.

"Yes, they've been briefed and whole heartily agree with our course of action. There will be no push back. Also, the Caswell unit is standing by waiting for your word."

Jewell nodded. "All right, you have a go. I want all of this done by tonight. We need to shut this down."

"It's done. Ah, sorry, Donovan. I know Hobbs is a friend. We just do not have another choice."

"I know," whispered Jewell, disconnecting the call. "I know."

***

Old money gated mansions and new money estates shared the woods on the border of Montgomery County, Maryland, and Fairfax County, Virginia, where brick driveways costing more than a quarter-million dollars turned off meandering roads through the upscale neighborhoods of Great Falls. For the casual observer driving through the area, the homes and estates were an example of the country-living real money could buy. The heavy wrought iron gates were in-your-face signposts announcing to those who didn't belong that looking was welcome but only from afar.

Hobbs had lived in one of these homes since 1979 and had raised two daughters on the sprawling ten-acre estate. A small creek ran the border of the property and reflected memories of his young girls catching crawdads and fireflies in jars. It had run in the background of their wedding photos taken on a manicured lawn under blue skies and sunshine.

For Hobbs, the home had always been a refuge, a place where the pressures and responsibilities faded away at the tall wrought iron gates. The estate was dark as he drove up, a reminder that his wife was still out of town at a business conference. He stopped his car near the front step and exited as he had a thousand times before, a comfortable domestic routine. He unlocked the double front door, stepped into the nearly dark house, and moved toward the newly renovated kitchen. An odd clicking sound coming from the hall behind him stopped him mid-stride. Before he could comprehend what he was seeing as he spun around, he was hit with a blinding green laser-light that physically knocked him backward sending him sprawling onto the newly tiled floor.

As he struggled to get to his feet, a massive flame shrouded apparition loomed up out of the darkness making him shriek in absolute terror. He fell back against the cabinets, too terrified to move as the fiery demon drifted closer. Beyond the horror he felt at seeing the shade, a sudden sharp pain began to radiate through his jaw and left arm, an intense pain that moved across his chest like a crushing vice. The steady pressure pushed the air out of his lungs in short desperate grunts.

His last conscious thought was that of his daughters playing beside the creek when they were young. With one last labored breath, there was nothing at all.

***

Twenty miles away, Antoine Palmari of the DC Metro Police was just finishing up his Big Mac and fries while sitting in his patrol car near the green line metro station downtown. He had come on at two in the afternoon and the shift had been too busy to catch a bite earlier. A year out of the academy and three years out of the Marine Corp, he was enjoying the challenge of police work. He was excited to be riding alone after breezing through his FTO (Field Training) in three months.

"Two Adam 40," announced his unit radio.

He picked up the mic, "Adam 40, go."

"Adam 40, we have a report of a possible hit and run with injuries at the intersection of 18th and P-street near Dupont circle. EMS is in route."

"Copy, In route." He turned on the lights and siren as he pulled away from the curb. As he drove through the city, he could hear other units responding to the call. Within minutes he was within sight of the scene. Several people were in the street frantically waving lit-up cell-phone screens in his direction.

Before he could get out of his unit, a young woman wearing a T-shirt covered with blood stains ran up to his door shouting something about a man needing an ambulance.

"Ma'am, step back," he shouted, getting out of his car. He pushed his way through a crowd of onlookers to see a man in bike shorts lying in the street, his body twisted and misshapened, a bicycle lying twenty yards away. Blood pooled thick and black around his head, glistening in the streetlight. A white water bottle and a shoe lay feet away, a clear indication of a fast-moving impact.

Palmari knelt to feel the man's neck for a pulse. He tried both sides and felt nothing.

"Did anyone see what happened here?" he asked as the EMS vehicle pulled up.

Three people began to speak at once.

"Hold on, one at a time. You Ma'am, what happened?"

"This dark green truck came down the street from that direction out of nowhere. It just ran right over the guy on the bike and kept on going."

"No shit!" announced the excited teenager standing beside her. "I just came out of the park and that truck was hauling ass, man. At least sixty. Tagged the dude and just kept rolling."

John Tolbert, Palmari's watch commander walked up as the medics began working on the man.

"What do we have?"

Palmari moved away from the crowd. "According to witness, sarge, the victim was run-down by a dark green or black pick-up that continued down P-street. I'm still trying to figure out who saw what."

Tolbert nodded. "Okay, let's put out a BOLO on the truck. Maybe someone will come across it." One of the medics stood up and covered the body with large yellow plastic and then walked over to the officers.

"We never got a pulse," he said peeling off his rubber gloves as several police units pulled in.

"Hey, guys," announced Tolbert as more officers walked up, "let's block off both ends of the street. This is a fatal. I'm going to turn this over to investigations." He turned back to Palmari. "Go ahead and get as many witness statements as you can. The investigators are going to want them."

"Sergeant, here's the guy's wallet," the second Medic announced as he walked up.

Crowds had now gathered on both sides of the street, drawn by the flashing blue lights and a chance to see the dead.

"Thanks, you can go ahead and clear. This is going to investigations as vehicular homicide."

"You got it," replied the medic. "I don't think the guy ever saw it coming. Ah, you sure you don't need us to stay?"

Talbert shook his head, "Go ahead and take off. The ME is on the way and we have more than enough people here to control the scene till the investigators show up."

"Okay, we'll grab our boxes and head out. Take care, Sarge."

As the medics loaded gear and prepared to leave, Talbert tucked his flashlight under his arm, allowing the beam to shine on the blood-stained wallet.

The name on the Maryland Driver's license was Caswell, Donald J, DOB 10/16/58. His attention alerted to the other ID card in the wallet, identifying Caswell Donald J as *Senior Director DIA*.

"Holy shit," he whispered. The investigation had just turned from a standard vehicular homicide case into a federal investigation. This could be the start of a major shit storm with national ramifications.

Minutes later Talbert was on the phone to the senior investigator in his division, the liaison officer to the feds, and dispatch looking to see if there had been any reports of the black or dark green pick-up truck related to the hit-and-run.

At that very moment, the truck in question was in a twenty-five-foot enclosed panel van ten miles west on its way to a crush and scrap yard just outside of Lexington, Kentucky, a facility used by the government for years. The black, 2014 Ford extended-cab truck would be a metal and plastic block half the size of a small refrigerator by morning. It would never be found.

To the men driving the truck, it was just another assignment in a long line of such operations. Orders were never questioned- never. DC had always been a tough town.

Epilogue

WASHINGTON POST   9/14/2018

There is shock and sadness in the halls of the United States Intelligence Services today with the news of the death of two of the Nation's top leaders in the field. George Hobbs, senior advisor to the President and National Intelligence Service Chief died of an apparent heart attack in his Great Falls' estate Saturday evening. Sources close to the investigation reported that Hobbs had been suffering from a heart condition for several years. He is survived by his wife and two daughters.

President Trump has expressed his sadness at the passing of Hobbs, stating that he was a "Great American and will be missed.' Politicians from both sides of the aisle have expressed sadness at Hobbs' passing, echoing the President's sentiments.

In a second incident, Donald Caswell of Reston Virginia was struck and killed Friday night while riding his bicycle in downtown DC. The accident has been listed as a hit and run. Authorities are looking for a black or green pickup truck in relation to this case. Caswell was the Senior Director of the Defense Intelligence Agency (DIA) and played a key role in forming a coalition of various government agencies against the war on terror during the Iraq and Afghanistan campaigns.

Caswell is survived by his wife. Metro police have urged the community to report any information they have concerning this case. A five thousand dollar reward has been offered for the capture and conviction of those responsible.

Jewell read the article again then folded the paper, tossing it in an empty chair as the waitress arrived with his plate of eggs, sausage, and hash browns.

"Here ya go," she announced, setting the plate down. "Can I get you anything else?"

Jewell smiled, "No, ma'am. I'm good. Thank you." Ted's Bulletin restaurant on 14th street was always open for breakfast. The food was good, the service fast, and the clientele mostly professional people who worked in the area, a convenient place for quick meetings within the beltway. Suits and ties were normal and no one batted an eye at seeing a senior congressman or senator ordering waffles and drinking coffee.

Jewell was well into his breakfast when Marcus Harper walked in and sat down across from him.

"Morning."

"Morning, Marcus. Did you read the paper?"

Harper poured a cup of coffee from the plastic carat. "Yes, I did. Terrible business. Sorry, Donovan. I know he was a close friend."

175

Jewell sat back in his chair with a sigh. "Well, what's done is done. How are we on implementation?"

"It is all in the control of our folks," replied Harper. "The enhanced array is at Langley, as directed. So, are we ready to start the program?"

Jewell looked around the room and then back at Harper and nodded. "After the midterms. We need to see what's going to happen with the House and Senate. If it does not go the way we think it should, we will start controlling the narrative."

Harper sipped his coffee and smiled. "Should be interesting."

THE END

Made in the USA
Monee, IL
22 January 2021